E.S.T.H.R.E.P.

EXTRA SOLAR TECHNOLOGICAL
HUMAN ROBOTIC EXPLORATION PROBE

ERIC WILKINS

Printed in New York by:

OMNIBOOK CO.
99 Wall Street, Suite 118
New York, NY 10005
USA
+1-866-216-9965
www.omnibookcompany.com

For e-book purchase: Kindle on Amazon, Barnes and Noble
Book purchase: Amazon.com, Barnes & Noble, and
www.omnibookcompany.com

Omnibook titles may be purchased in bulk for educational, business, fund-raising, or sales promotional use. For more information please e-mail info@omnibookcompany.com

CONTENTS

ESTHREP'S LAUNCH

APRIL 12 2143

CHAPTER 1
ESTHREP'S DESTINATION

The name Sirius from ancient times, is derived from a Greek word meaning sparkling or scorching.

Sirius is sometimes called the Dog Star.

The Sirius system, also called Alpha Canis Majoris or the Dog Star, is one of the brightest stars in the night sky. It's a binary star in the constellation of Canis Major and its approximate visual magnitude is 1.46.from Earth.

The system is a unique binary double star system in the constellation of Canis Major

The bright component of the binary pair is a blue-white star system that is 25.4 times as luminous as our faithful Sun.

Sirius A's radius is 1.71 times that of Earth's Sun, which means it is more than double the mass of our solar system's star the Sun.

Sirius has a surface temperature of 9,940 kelvins, which equates to 17,432 degrees Fahrenheit and is more than 4,000 K higher or hotter 6740 Fahrenheit) than Earth's life giving star.

The Sirius system's distance from our solar system is approximately 8.6 light-years and more than twice the distance to the nearest known star system known as the Alpha Centaury.

A beam of light travels 5,878 and a half, billion miles in a years time.

Esthrep traveling at half light speed would require two years to travel one light years distance.

It had now taken the Esthrep Probe, 18 years to begin to be within 20 days arrival time of entering the early bow shock wave of the Huge Sirius Star System.

Presently from Mar's Base, other probes were being proposed, built and scheduled to be launched to several other nearby star systems.

But, the purpose here is to reveal the unfolding secrets and journey chronicles of the Esthrep Sirius adventure.

You are humbly invited to open your imaginative creative minds, and join this journey as facts of the Chronicles of Esthrep's - Journey to Sirius are soon revealed.

CHAPTER 2
THE ESTHREP PROBE

The Esthrep Probe is neither male nor female in its basic total entity, but in ever-trueful essence, it equally contained equal attributes of both female and male human species of planet Earth.

The probe itself, is a self-aware human combined technological robotic exploration probe of humanities latest attempt at gaining more astronomy knowledge.

The Esthrep One Probe was the first such mission to be launched to another star.

Sirius was chosen first over Alpha Centuri because a decade ago, astronomers had discovered FRB (fast radio burst) frequency pulses that had suddenly began and occurred repeatedly without ceasing before Esthrep's launch to the Sirius system.

It was indeed a curiosity that had to be investigated first over the closer Alpha Centuri system.

Esthrep is a extremely smart well equipped twentieth second century technological achievement of many great scientific minds and extraordinary space vehicle builders from several of the best space corporation firms of its then launch era of 2143.

The probe is a marvelous exploration machine combined with human intelligent intervention.

Esthrep the probe's sleek triangle steel blue outer edges, softly glowed in the deep cold darkness of the space as Esthrep sailed its determined very important sojourn.

At precise 3.14 second intervals, Esthrep's main nuclear ion engines fired soft blue pulses of propulsion blast.

All three sides of the probe's half-kilometer long base, rotated gracefully revolving clockwise forward at a 3.14 second rotation rate.

For nearly two decades, the larger main frame Esthrep had dutifully traversed the journey towards it's intended destination of Sirius with its six passengers pods tucked safely away and studiously protected by Esthrep and maintained in a deep cold stasis sleep.

CHAPTER 3
THE AWAKENING BEGINS

Days away from the approach of the bow shock wave as presently viewed from above the 5 meter diameter lead Esthrep Main Commander, the probe sailed forward emitting its ultraviolet blue V bat like entity in the deep black cold ocean void of space.

The six one-meter diameter human conscious globes rested contently in frozen suspended animation totally in slumber to time's measured of the two-decade passage.

The six globe inhabitants each rode their globe half imbedded and equal spaced on two sides of Esthrep's triangle configuration.

Twenty years of deep cold tedious uneventful travel with Esthrep main frame at the control while traveling half the speed of light or 93,000 miles traveled for every second that continuously passed.

Along the two sides of Esthrep's triangular profile, there were three even spaced meter sized orbs that softly began pulsing while riding three each wing with the larger five meter globe called Esthrep Main, was commandingly riding near the forward tip of Esthrep's V shaped configuration.

Each of the six human dna orbs began flashing gentle pulses and releasing steamed gasses of neon colors into space as the ship's nuclear ion engines silently stopped spinning and projected reverse blue flames in the opposite direction of the probe's destination vector.

Esthrep was thawing its six modules simultaneously while decreasing speed in order to meet the Sirius Bow Shock Wave that existed 20 earth day rotations time ahead.

CHAPTER 4

MORE ABOUT SIRIUS A

Sirius A is about twice as massive as Earth's Sun and has an absolute visual magnitude of +1.42 from Earth

Sirius A is also 25 times more luminous than our Sun but has a significantly lower luminosity than other brighter stars.

It's presently estimated that The Sirius system's age is between 200 and 300 million years old. It is also speculated that the Sirius system was originally composed of two bright bluish stars.

The more massive of these, Sirius B, consumed its fuel resources rapidly and became a red giant before shedding its outer layers and collapsing into its current state as a white dwarf around 120 million years ago.

A white dwarf star is a star that has burned most of its fuel and is now shrunken and compressed down to an earth sized body that is still very hot

Approximately 8.6 light years from Earth, exist a double solar system called Sirius A and B, that now awaited Esthrep and crew's exploration.

Now star date of 10232162, newly learned knowledge about the little known double star solar system was being assimilated and stored in Esthrep's computer banks. Hopefully, Earth's Human Race would one day gain future knowledge from the Esthrep Exploration Probe. .

Knowledge thus far, only knew that the Sirius system to be the double sun Dog Star named Sirius A and B

Legend had it that creatures of Sirius had long ago visited Earth and changed humans evolution to a revolutionary awakening.

Many such legends also revealed connections to the building of the pyramids in ancient Earth's history.

Sailing silently through space, Esthrep and its six smaller orbs cryogenically continued thawing as Esthrep captained the long journey that awaits their arrival. Esthrep's main frame five meter diameter orb captained and controlled all functions of its journey from the probe's forward tip.

CHAPTER 5
ESTHREP MAIN AND 6 ORBS

Six entity globes riding three each wing rested half exposed protruding above the triangle shaped wings.

Esthrep's four nuclear Ion engines pulsed fiery rays of silent propulsion in space.

The probe's mainframe was uniquely merged with all six. Each globe was a separate dna human embodied entity. Each contained the DNA essence of a revived consciousness entity. They were six of Earth's chosen best considered minds both past and present.

That is, at the time of Esthrep's launch date of April twelfth, twenty one forty three from Mars orbital base station.

Esthrep's main computer was itself, a self aware robotic entity in lead command control of the probe's main functions and navigation systems. Esthrep was always responsible for keeping the six crew members safe. The orbs were always in its charge and kept protected in their stasis orbs safe and sound.

Esthrep had began slowing down while approaching its intended destination.

CHAPTER 6
KATTIE WILLIAMS TECHNOLOGY

Aboard the Esthrep Probe, were three male and three female self-aware conscious entities that each occupied their own separate liquid stasis chamber inside a clear round ceramic one meter diameter liquid amino acid core globe.

Each human conscious chip and their human emulated entity, were always directly linked to Esthrep's main computer memory bank of information.

The number one, two and three ceramic embodiment computer chips, were the disembodied remaining consciousness of three male renowned respected scientist of a past Earth era.

The 4, 5 and 6 orbs, were three female scientist DNA entities embodied in their orbs.

Humanity and technology had changed tremendously in the year twenty one forty one, when a bright young genius biochip engineering student from Cornell University named Kattie Williams, discovered a specific technique to revive and inject a humans DNA consciousness, inside a meter diameter filled liquid super molecular amino acid globe in the form of an advanced super computer chip.

The age of the super macro chip revolutionized humanity and nations had began to seriously cease their warring ways and began concentrating on repairing major ecological damage caused from past human abuse to our fragile grand spaceship Earth.

Individuals now had the ability to alloy their spirit consciousness inside a macro chip whenever the body was worn out and no longer able to function biologically.

Holographic communication from the afterlife helped humanity to better deal with stressful loss of life situations and opened the door to new grand possibilities of human consciousness traveling along with robotic exploration probes to neighboring star systems.

CHAPTER 7
ESTHREP MAIN'S ENTITY, CARL SAGAN

(November 9, 1934 - December 20, 1996)

Carl Edward Sagan was born on November 9, 1934, in Brooklyn, New York, the first of two children.

Sagan's interest in astronomy began early on, and when he was five, his mother sent him to the library to find books on the stars.

In 1955, Sagan graduated with a B.A. in physics, and he received his masters a year later.

It was his DNA that is injected into Esthrep's main frame and the six orbs upon awaken completion, would experience it all at the same instant that Esthrep comprehended each moment.

CHAPTER 8
ESTHREP'S LONG AGO MEMORIES

As the most recent great conjunction of Sirius A and B had occurred around 2013. A wave of freedom was sweeping Planet Earth that culminated in the breakdown of all the Communist rule in Europe and the second liberation of the cold war had finally ended these events transpiring simultaneously with the magnetic forces building to there highest intensity on Sirius. Perhaps there may be a connection.

It was at this exact moment along the time continuum, that Esthrep's home planet Earth and Mars base was a distant long ago memory.

Simply a static visual of a precious water blue world floating gracefully in Esthrep's random access memory projection, appearing as if it was suspended by a single invisible thread two thirds of the way from the center of our own Milky Way Galaxy.

Esthrep was the first interstellar outbound exploration probes launched from Earth's historical era of 2143 and for 20 earth years sailing it patiently traversed the blackness of the eight point six light years distance from Earth at one half light speed.

CHAPTER 9

BOW SHOCK WAVE ENCOUNTER AHEAD

Now, star date April third 2162, Esthrep began a slow oscillation orientation maneuver to begin the preparation of firing its super engine thrusters in order to further slow down from a swift forward speed of 93,120 miles traveled every second.

Pyrotechnic bolts exploded and three circular three meter sized panels simultaneously fell away as a coned metallic shield deployed causing Esthrep to morph into a burning tip arrow as it began engaging the approaching star systems bow shockwave head on while deflecting the hot gaseous dust particles around its swift forward path.

Three nuclear explosive engines spat pulsed anti- matter propulsion burst in an opposite direction of their unfurled position and in a span of several continuous hours of retro fire, had accomplished decelerating Esthrep's speed velocity down to one tenth light speed or 18,628 miles traveled forward for ever second of time that elapsed.

CHAPTER 10
SIRIUS DOG STAR'S ANCIENT LEGEND.

Ancient legend records, that a tribe from Earth's Ancient West African Continent was visited by beings from a planet from the habitable zone of the Sirius Dog Star System.

The Sirius name came from the Greek word searing or scorching. Canis Major the greatest dog representing Orion's larger hunting pack is commonly referred to as The Dog Star Sirius.

CHAPTER 11
BOW SHOCK ENCOUNTER ORDEAL

A triangular, bug eyed ceramic skinned robotic probe morphed and tucked three tentacles rearward as an electric force field shroud formed around Esthrep's head as it began interacting deeper plunging violently with the outer dust filled gaseous bow shock wave at the extreme edge of this never by humans explored Sirius A and B solar system.

The probe began vibrating extremely and suddenly a loud pop occurred and then echoed away into silence as the Esthrep Probe gracefully sailed into a magical place where physics presently existed differently upon an all new unique forms of nature's delightful expression.

Now exposed, Esthrep sailed silently into a extravagant three star system where possibly other life forms could exist.

Somewhere in this neighboring Dog Star system, there may exist life similar to life from our own Solar System. Perhaps even an intelligent species.

Esthrep realized that the Probe was the alien here and it had dutifully activated its defenses.

Still slowly awakening, were the six meter sized imbedded globe orbs that were evaporating the last of their frozen vapors into space. Esthrep Main continued the thawing process of it's goal of heating all globes up to approximately 98 degrees Fahrenheit. That process would take 48 more Earth hours.

Indeed Esthrep had memories of Mars construction and the humans that built and launched this probe. But, it couldn't within its own survival mode begin to comprehend a reason at present to remember or access that irreverent past information.

A long ago implanted repeating echo of a simple guidance code would forever guide its compulsion to explore this new territory.

Although warm-blooded human abilities were forbidden to possibly ever tread this far.

Kattie Williams dna human intelligence implant discovery in 2141 made the Esthrep probe possible.

This emissary robotic craft had journeyed ever so patiently across a lonely dark abyss to this systems comet filled icy edge as it gracefully began deploying huge solar panels and arraying them star-wards towards Sirius A to begin a vital process of recharging its nearly depleted back up fuel cell battery power source near the center of its structure.

CHAPTER 12
COLOSSUS THE COLD SUN

Esthrep had safely broken through the bow shock barrier but was still approximately two hundred light hours distance or well over ninety Earth astronomical units from the Tri-Star's system center rotation point.

It now calculated that precisely at its present approach speed of 11,160 kilometers per second, it would arrive at the newly discovered Colossus C on the outer edge of this solar system in three hours and fifteen minutes from this instance along the time continuum.

The electrons in Esthrep's futuristic solar panels began circulating fast bytes of solar charged particles as they sped sporadically along the gold soldered vanes and circuit boards inside all the probes silver blue ceramic body.

Calculations and computations of past present and future began configuring simultaneously into Esthrep's present state of awareness.

Super energizing power engulfed Esthrep's entire being as it became aware that this was an energy source of a type that it had never experience before.

Suddenly, Esthrep became aware of a whispering message from somewhere deep within a concealed quadrant and was immediately informed through its precision tuned sensor probes of an immanent approaching danger.

Esthrep violently burst through the inner bow-shock ice dust cloud and all three of it's nuclear engines spat a stream of reverse fire igniting in a furious attempt of further slowing it's swift forward speed.

The onboard video screen simultaneously projected a magnified visual to all chips aboard of a huge gigantic fast rotating frozen ice star system ahead.

Esthrep immediately took evasive action and its engines gimbaled away from the tremendous gravity influences of the approaching spinning crackling cold ice world and it's many moons.

A visual of nine multi-colored planetoids orbited an icy megalith world on the very edge of this Sirius system and now labeled a three star class C system.

Esthrep began to conserve its remaining nuclear fuel supply instinctively vectoring toward a safer orbit in a moon swept out zone inward of a trailing falling comet ice storm and then Esthrep swiftly fell in behind the largest planetoid moons orbit.

C's diameter was 600,000 miles and its twelve planetoid moons ranged in size from 700 kilometers, to 5,000 kilometers in diameter which was the size of the largest planetoid moon that Esthrep was presently decelerating behind into a safe observation orbit.

CHAPTER 13
THE TITUS MOON

Esthrep's eight trailing legs simultaneously began deploying from their reverse fold, then began flexing their joints and extending probe sensor tips barely forward of the center heart of its forward motion.

A devilish rusty red moon now titled Titus, projected upon Esthrep's forward view screen as the volcanic large body rotated swiftly at a 96-degree angel to C's equator and spat numerous volley plumes of hot orange nitrous-oxide and methane fire high into it's poisonous atmosphere.

Hundreds of fire volleys escaped gravity and some fell towards the Colossus Cold Sun first freezing, then crystallizing into rusty rosy snowballs of fire ice with a burning hot inner core falling towards the cold sun that this hot Moon orbited.

The cold sun was actually sucking in heat from the coldness of absolute zero.

Extreme static lightning bolts violently discharged cloud to surface and surface to clouds saturating the toxic moon's atmosphere with a super static tingling reverberation flash of spectral charged lights as Esthrep passed above it's north pole.

Many of the furious dirty fireballs didn't reach escape velocity and ultimately splattered back to the red hot boiling fast rotating moon's surface.

Esthrep watched as the rolling remaining burning destructive fireballs finally exploded upon impact with an already eat out leaning elevated mountain peak. Many high mountain ranges jutted jagged teeth skyward over 10 kilometers high into the moons electrically charged volatile atmosphere.

Esthrep sailed gracefully on past the red moon's body then focused its attention towards the huge crackling ice Sirius-C cold star that was presently approximately forty five thousand miles away and almost as big as the Earth's Sun.

CHAPTER 14

COLOSSUS C IN PASSING

Esthrep had duly recorded this extremely weird heavenly body's name as Colossus-C

It's huge diameter was approximately 600,000 miles

Colossus C, was a Jovial sized compressed ice world with a mass equaling approximately 93 percent of our Sun but this world was almost our hot suns diameter.

The probes exploration speed had now been reduced to 65,000 miles per hour or 19 miles per. second and at that speed it would take the probe two more Earth days to reach Colossus-C.

The immense gravitational tug at the center of Titus's fast rotating core caused this orbiting moon to be highly volcanically active deep down kilometers below the surface while churning it's core like a hot blender causing the moon to project a compressed electrically charged magnetic field in the clockwise orbital direction all the way around it's super cold giant C host star.

Esthrep fell inward around the immense gravity well of the colossus C, vectoring its nuclear engines toward an anticipated slingshot maneuver that would hurl it deeper inward toward a waiting to be explored Sirius B system that was still concealed in the intense glare of the larger hot Sirius A Star.

Its eight spider tipped probes focused in on the Colossus C crackling ice world as it fell around the outer edge of its massive slingshot gravity grip.

Visuals of horrendous landslide waves of crystal frozen exotic matter the size of mountains bashed against vast frosty frozen metallic shorelines. The waves then receded gradually backward. The giant waves of receding cold matter eventually met other opposite waves causing a third inner wave that emitted a very peculiar radio frequency static charge signal at the moment that the third wave peaked with the secondary wave crest.

Dark dirty comets of all sizes continuously crashed into Colossus's shadowy backside creating cold static lightning bolts that ricocheted skyward dissipating into beautiful rainbow colored burst of electrically charged energy that sparkled and trailed toward the stars brighter side reflection.

Sirius C's surface temperature was actually colder than the cold space environment of its orbit.

It was determined that Colossus C was deliberately sucking static cold charges directly from the environment of space itself.

Somehow, Colossus's temperature was below the measurable scale of absolute zero.

As cold as space is, Colossus was undetectable by astronomers from Earth and it was somehow sucking heat from the absolute zero temperature of space itself.

Upon deeper analysis, Esthrep discovered that the majority of comet matter that fell into this cold world mostly consisted of iron metal matter and in fact, Colossus C itself had a huge metallic core that made up sixty three percent of its entire mass.

Colossus C was indeed a large iron core cold star approximately six hundred thousand miles in diameter and Esthrep now calculated that this outer system orbited the A and B inner stars on a parabolic oval orbit once every five hundred and seventy nine Earth years.

It reflected very little of the light that it received from the bright Sirius A and B Stars that was now well over 80 earth AU's inward.

Deep penetrating radar echoes revealed that 100 kilometers below the surface, the temperature became extremely colder than the already frozen super cold surface.

Esthrep played a recording of the sounds emanating from Colossus's surface at the same frequency pitch of humans limited hearing range.

Sirius C emitted a sound of musical crashing granular harmonic waves echoing thunderous quaking rumbles as its heavy gravity tossed its oceanic rolling frozen matter towards eat out metal mountains.

The matter erupting in super bright flashes of electrically charge lightning bolts upon arrival at the crest of the extremely battered mountainous shoreline.

Brilliant orange-red monstrous vapor clouds filled the horizon of Colossus's dusk as they sailed onward towards the now setting in the east Sirius A star. It was indeed a visual sequence that any great Earth artist could ever aspire to achieve.

CHAPTER 15
ON TO SIRIUS B

For the first time now through the dust filtered spectral light of the setting Sirius C Star, Esthrep could distinctly momentarily detect the infamous small hidden presence of the Sirius B Star.

It calculated Sirius B's diameter to be approximately twelve thousand kilometers and its orbit around Sirius A to be, once every sixty nine point eight earth years time.

Eureka warnings rang out as its x-ray spectral probes faintly detected at least three new planets in orbit around the Sirius B star system.

Calculations were quickly estimated from probabilities that the largest of these three worlds was possibly an earth size planet in the habitable zone around the Sirius B system.

Long range scanners were still struggling to discern many details yet and ships sensors were still millions of kilometers distance and many hours travel away from these inner orbiting rocky bodies.

Only time would reveal many more details about these wondrous worlds yet to explore.

The crews chatter echoed through the communications channels of the ships main fluid core as they all rejoiced the journey's news thus far and all the new details.

It was certain that the Earth size planet in the distant habitable zone ahead filled the main content of their excited converse.

Extreme magnified images of the Earth sized world faintly revealed a whisky clouded planet with shades of pale greenish brown in it's still hard to discern details.

CHAPTER 16

ESKALON THREE AHEAD

Colossus C was now fading in the distance but the cold star was still a formidable presence in the rear visual monitor.

Esthrep and crew ventured ahead swiftly inward towards the awaiting worlds of discovery in this remarkable three star sun system.

As the distance slowly calibrated downward towards the three inner worlds of the Sirius B system, the first outer rocky planet was due to be reached in one hour and fifty minutes earth time period.

Forward sensors were picking up signs of a five thousand kilometer diameter outer yellow world with six asteroid sized moons.

Two of the moons were between three and four hundred kilometer diameter while the other four moons were odd shaped orbiting bodies between three and twenty five kilometers in diameter and they were very odd sized shaped rolling bodies.

This dancing system of heavenly moon bodies orbited the planet ranging from one million kilometers at their apogee and 450 thousand kilometers at their closest perigee approach.

Sirius B orbited a twenty thousand earth day revolve around the center gravity of Sirius A.

That's almost 55 Earth Years.

It was such a spectacular sight to behold as the crew eagerly anticipated more facts of the approaching mysterious worlds.

Esthrep and crew were close enough now to measure the outer sixth moon.

It's gravity measured twenty eight percent earth gravity and it's atmosphere consisted mostly of nitrogen and sulfur mixed with approximately ten percent carbon dioxide and very little oxygen content that registered on Esthrep's forward deep sensors.

Oxygen was present but it measured less than one tenth of one percent.

Total atmospheric surface pressure was only about one percent earth pressure at sea level. Surface temperature at the equator measured approximately two hundred below zero on the Fahrenheit scale.

Soon Esthrep and crew would fly by this system at closest approach. The Moon was now dubbed Eskalon three as its new name that was quickly debated and decided on by the crew giving the moon a new title.

Eskalon's moons were titled to it's equatorial orbital plane and titled alphabetically starting with the largest down to the smallest, A through F.

The Probe sailed just a few thousand kilometers above the icy white moon surface vectoring on inward towards Planet Eskalon the first encountered main body in this system that measured approximately eight thousand kilometers in diameter or 4,970 miles.

This magnificent world ahead had an orange amber gold tint that is mixed with scattered dark green swirl clouds in it's upper atmosphere.

Dutifully, Esthrep's sensor recorders tallied the information away in its computer banks as the vital statistics as the approaching marble world gave more details.

Now was the time that Esthrep's main computers were linked directly to the crews consciousness.

No one needed to speak. All information was directed to the six in real time as Esthrep experienced reality.

The six were linked directly to Esthrep's robotic intelligence and they all functioned together as if they were all one in the same as Esthrep's main computer brain.

Eskalon's details were revealing a world with twenty eight percent Earth gravity and a only a eleven percent iron core.

It's rotation rate was one rotation ever eight hours and ten minutes earth time making it's day and night cycle each about four hours and five minutes. It revolved around Sirius B at a distance of a 250 million kilometers or 155 million miles and orbited the Earth sized star Sirius B, approximately once every three earth years.

It's mostly cold upper nitrogen atmosphere consisting of eighty percent carbon dioxide and the rest showing traces of methane in the upper swirled cloud tops.

The surface at the equator was a cold ninety below zero Fahrenheit.

Total atmospheric pressure measured approximately sixty five millibars compared to earth's one thousand millibars at sea level.

A grand group of cold worlds indeed, were these orbiting group of heavenly bodies that danced their journey along a trodden path in the distant that they revolved.

Esthrep had chosen to track the outside orbit of these dancing outer worlds and now used the system of worlds gravity to vector them inward towards a promising inner world in the apparent goldilocks zone of the two orbiting Sirius A and B stars ahead.

The entire Esthrep probe fell further inward now leaving Eskalon and the pack of cold moon worlds behind as the use of Esthrep's main engines vectored the entire crew towards a celestial blue iced capped world in the long range visual display for all to review.

A new destination now was some distance away but Esthrep's engines maneuvered to hasten the journey time by forty percent.

Arrival time at the new planet was estimated to be twenty eight earth hours away.

Esthrep's gain of speed also required a reverse thrusts maneuver at the two hour mark of the now beginning new journey.

All that was discerned at this point and distance, is that the mostly blue planet ahead was approximately eleven thousand kilometers or 6,835 miles in diameter and the planet appeared to have two major three thousand kilometer moons. Time and distance would soon reveal the details of the traversing adventure ahead.

It was revealed that the crew's modules were stressed from the past adventures and therefore a type of sleep mode was induced to the crew as their minds would need to be fresh when the details were revealed about the new destination ahead.

They slept as Esthrep's computer mind tallied away at monitoring the ships status and entire well being of all as the crew gained much needed down time.

Their generation pods only allowed their consciousness for a limited amount of time before the pod itself would go into a regeneration state as the occupant entered a dream state rest period.

Much to their individual anticipation, they awaited with ease the hours of distance to be traversed in a relaxed dream sleep mode.

Each to their own dream state, their entities individually stored the gained information and their computer minds defragmenter to make room for much more awaiting hours of discovery.

Esthrep main patiently alert at the control panel steady calculated the progress and distance to be traversed. Esthrep main is the only member of the crew that had a back up regenerator module that allowed it to be alert for many long hours.

Along the long journey here although in stasis, each of the other individuals orbs were reactivated one at a time, and took turns monitoring Esthrep's progress while Esthrep Main itself shut down and regenerated for a period of two earth days.

Esthrep was not an organic individual identity like the six earth aliens aboard. It was indeed a much larger sophisticated computer that controlled and protected the entire probe and its crew. But, It's larger Orb was injected with the DNA of Carl Sagan to mesh with its sophisticated computer entity's mind.

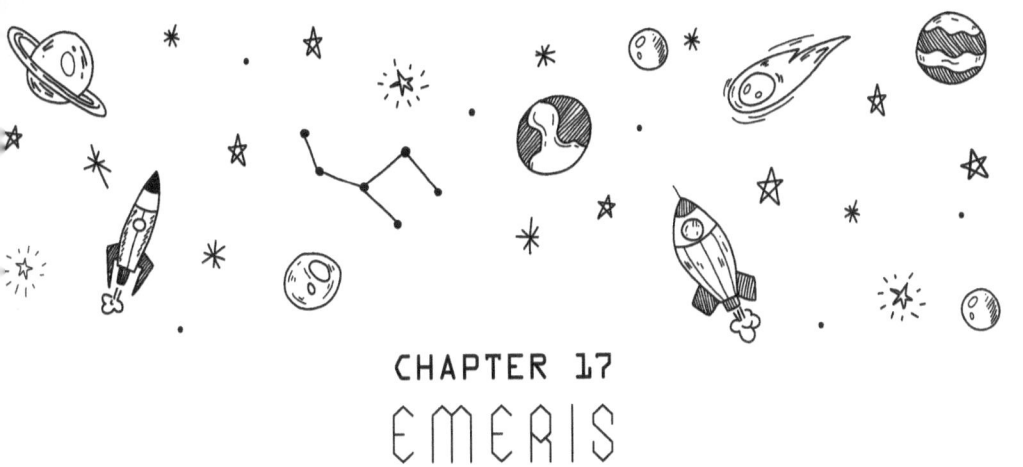

CHAPTER 17
EMERIS

The Probe's engines decreased the crafts forward speed as the orbital velocity required to orbit the approaching world would be reached in about five hours and two minutes.

The six revived from stasis sleep began to link in on the approaching beautiful multi colored planet magnified in the ships viewer screen.

At this distance, it's white polar snow caps had a tinge of pale blue as the brown and green land masses appeared as huge islands that were sometimes linked in various peculiar shapes and textures.

A type of thick gelatin liquid light blue sea surrounded all the land masses that had the appearance of a pasty darker brown-bluish color.

As Esthrep approached at a slowing orbital velocity, only thirty percent of the planet was lit from the Earth sized star's light.

Esthrep fell into the dark side of the planet and it's engines ignited with furious thrust to slow down to obtain proper orbital speed for a fall around orbit.

Esthrep was now a thousand kilometers or just over 600 miles above the surface on the night side and now fell gracefully behind the new world into a proper oblong orbit. Esthrep now witnessed a rearward beautiful star set scene. It was a two moon crescent evening of this beautiful new world with two moons showing in the distance.

Two stars were visible. One far away very bright white yellow star and one closer tinted light red star beautifully lit the early view of this world entitled Emeris confirmed immediately by Esthrep and the crew.

ESTHREP

Emeris was approximately eleven thousand kilometers or a little under 6800 miles in diameter at its equator, with two shimmering colorful moons orbiting this fast rotating world.

It's rotation rate was 12 hours and twenty minutes, meaning that it's day and night cycles were each about six hours and ten minutes long.

Esthrep's orbital speed was only slightly faster than Emeris rotation speed.

Therefore, the probe approached the day side slowly and viewed the surface below under a double star exploration's first ever view.

The probe did wonder if there was intelligent life on this smaller earthlike world or were they all soon to meet other intelligent worlders?

The moments approached as Esthrep launched mini probes ahead of the ship to detect any signs of communication satellites or any known types of civilization to be detected.

Scanners were detecting surface temperatures ranging from below zero Fahrenheit to a moderate ninety degree temperature at the fast rotating equator.

Quite Earthlike to be precise, but there were extreme unique differences.

Here was a world 20 percent smaller than earth's size with a surface gravity that measured approximately 58 percent of earth's gravity,

Certainly a less massive body but it's liquid water content was only half the volume that Planet Earth contained.

Thicker gel-like waters covered approximately 40 percent of the entire Emeris surface.

The lands between were huge fractured continents many joined and many floating on spiral scribbled sands with large misty forest growth spanning the fast rotating equator.

The bands of forest growth spiraled in swirls upward and downward in rotating bands until fading out towards the frosted white poles past rotation at both ends of this gorgeous globe. It appeared as a beautiful Christmas ornament hanging in the blackness of space.

Esthrep burst into a first pinkish sunrise of the B star. A few more seconds pasted as more surface became visible below in a dark rose sunlight until it gave way to the very sudden bright rays of Sirius A's yellow white starlight. B's light was now almost invisible and lost in the glare of Sirius A.

No signs were detected yet of any known communication signals but Esthrep was now detecting a peculiar low tone on the tectonic vibration music scale.

The signal's pulse seemed to be based on a reverberation scale of six equaling one base unit to earths ten based system.

Esthrep and crew were feverishly trying to decode the low frequency tone signal that seemed to be emanating from about 17 degrees north of the planet's equator .

The base reverberation code of six was quickly becoming the entire crews major task of deciphering to see if there was possibly a decodable intelligent message attached.

More surface detail became available as Esthrep sensors acclimated to the new world environment below.

Atmospheric details revealed a pressure of six hundred, ninety five millibars compared to Earth's pressure of one thousand millibars

Double shadowed gray blue clouds swirled the equator region chasing the fast rotation of Emeris.

Two stars casting separate directional angles caused the gorgeous Emeris planet to shimmer double shadows upon the lands and seas below the now orbiting Esthrep Probe and crew.

It produced an awe inspiring sight..

As the ship approached the night side, twinkling electrical auroras beautified the poles of Emeris

Indeed, very valuable information was already conceived of this planet system's biography expediently being stored in Esthrep's data banks to be treasured forever and some day relayed back to Earth.

CHAPTER 18
MOONS OF EMERIS

The entire crew's fascination then diverted their attention to the planets two Moons.

Studiously named by the Crew as Erathuis and Arris the description quickly followed.

Erathuis was a very heavy cratered gray moon similar to Earth's moon in reflection and it orbited at an approximate distance of 300 thousand kilometers or 186,000 miles above Emeris and took almost 35 Earth day measurements to orbit the planet once.

It was also tidally locked one side always facing Emeris in its orbit.

Now, Arris was a different Moon entirely. It orbited Emeris at a closer seventy four thousand miles or 120 thousand kilometers, once every 14 earth days and also rotated very fast once every 67 Earth minutes.

Arris was a small black carbon moon that was 550 miles in diameter or approximately 770 kilometers.

It's surface was extremely hot for such a small moon and the darkness below was a cooking tar pit of carbon molten liquid.

Temperatures ranging from 170 degrees Fahrenheit at the poles to 390 F degrees at the equator.

Arris was continuously being squeezed and stretched by the fast oblong orbit around Emeris

Pools of dark hot boiling tar continually gurgled and boiled over almost the entire surface only to be separated by the tips of orange lines of a single remaining mountain tip peak.

The entire small moon appeared as a black ball with hot orange fragmented magma lines spiraling the molten surface. Its low gravity allowed the bubbling hot tar to be propel fire globs ten meters high from boiling tar pits before cooling and slowly falling back to the surface with a slow motion splash.

As the Esthrep crew continued discovering the three body system Esthrep's crew issued the command to obtain a closer orbit of 280 kilometers or approximately 170 miles above the beautiful Emeris equator.

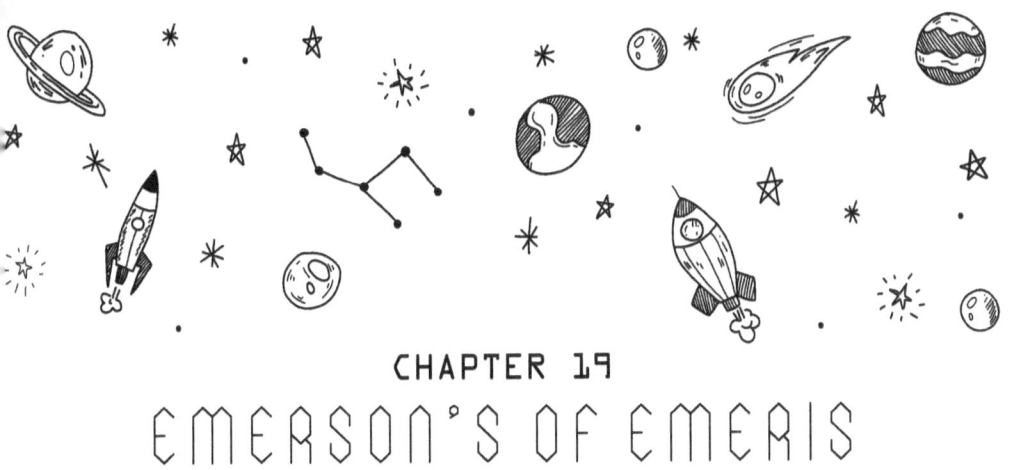

CHAPTER 19
EMERSON'S OF EMERIS

Esthrep sensors again were suddenly picking up the low frequency bass signals it had received earlier.

Now the signal became tenfold stronger.

The crew and Esthrep's computers were struggling feverishly to decipher if it was possibly an intelligent signal or not.

Finally, a decipher code was discovered and they were able to break the code of the Emeris signal message below. It was indeed an Erika moment.

A civilization was detected.

There were beings detected and computers worked at an accelerated pace to decipher the message from this new life form.

Also detected below were rivers of flowing thick waters. There were water channels spiraling north and southward between vegetated spirals of land plant growth.

These land spirals flowing waterways, are where the inhabitants of this world lived among floating barrel like rotating homes.

Huge rotating cylinders floated buoyant with most of the cigar shaped structure below the water line.

Streams steadily flowing at 50 kilometers per hour were transporting families of these beings around the globe north and south around Emeris.

First contact was about to occur. Esthrep and crew issued greetings and peaceful intentions and waited anxiously for a reply.

Fragmented translations began to reveal a pleasant but cautious response and welcome.

A map of planet co ordinance and a specific welcome destination was marked for immediate first contact consideration.

First was revealed details of humans of our Planet Earth to their species and messages were sent back and forth to the Emerson's of Emeris.

Translation at first was slow but as Esthrep's computers caught on to short hand of their code, it soon became possible to communicate on a ten minute delay with the Emeris beings.

These crustaceous beings dwelled inside their rolling floating cylinders partially submerged in Emeris flowing river waters. Inside the cylinders, it didn't rotate at all. Their technology was fascinating and their world was all that they knew of until now.

Not yet into space exploration but certainly very intelligent in many unique ways.

Ceramic earth bowl beings from Earth were very strange to the Emerson's.

They couldn't seem to quite comprehend the fact that the earth species that were incased aboard the probe in their chemical bio containment units, was an invented technology to allow space exploration.

They understood the framework of the human body but the concept of having their DNA revived and traveling the stars was a technology completely foreign to their present existence.

They the Emerson's had developed sophisticated technology for their world. Everything was unique to the Emeris way of life.

Energy was harnessed from the double stars and pollution was a thing that was beyond their comprehension.

Each home was self sufficient and also harnessed the rolling traversing waves to produce power.

They had voices of low bass mimicking clicking sounds to communicate.

They sounded very similar to dolphin clicking sounds of Earth but had a much lower bass tone that was so low it vibrated softly like an Earth bass speaker.

The surface pressure on Emeris was about 58 percent of Earth's atmospheric pressure. Gravity on this world was about 53 percent Earth gravity.

The flowing rivers were always propelled by the gravitational pull of the two moons and two stars.

Emeris's yearly cycle was approximately 400 earth days around Sirius B but their planet rotated once every 12 hours and twenty minutes. Making their day night cycles about six hours and ten minutes each. Their year had about sixteen hundred rotation cycles as their planet Emeris revolved around   Sirius B once in its year.

How to describe these strange new Emeris beings is a casual thing that is best described in Earth terms as meter long crustaceous creatures somewhat greenish yellow in color.

Their perception of up and down was somewhat limited due to the horizontal flowing nature of their existence in their always moving river homes.

No creature on Earth resembled these Emeris beings but the closest thing to it would be dolphin like creatures except that these Emerson's besides having multible fins, had one arm-like feature projecting from its center body about a half meter in length with two elbow like bending joints with 6 tiny like finger grabbings that were amazing to watch their precision tiny finger movements.

They communicated between their species in ways the earthlings were very amused at their playful banter. They somewhat sounded like baby infants laughing as they always moved in random vectors and never collided.

Their center body arm always pointing the way they wished to commute but their mystical fingers always deciding a fraction of an Earth second ahead to deviate from their intended coarse.

It's hard to attempt to explain this unique society of peaceful beings on this beautiful world.

At times in their individual movements, they'd tuck their arm inward while resting for minutes at a time.

They each existed in a continuous cycle of work minutes and rest minutes. During brief rest periods, their bodies would vibrate and purr as if being recharged for the coming awakening cycle.

They were quick to awaken and went straight to the next cycles task of their amazing worlds peaceful existence.

Their minds had no way to know or hate such as in wars. Their world had never had a war. Although some existed of different skin tones, most were the colors mentioned earlier. They had two walnut-shaped eyes that darted quickly around in their always searching movement.

Their society were mostly vegetarian but they did ingest a steak like meaty substance several times during their short awake periods.

Strange as it may be, their family societies lived a dozen or so a dwelling inside their rolling river constructed homes.

These amazing creatures sometimes took quick excursions outside their dwellings to communicate with local neighbors and quickly returned to their personal families quarters.

Water creatures with tail like fins and gills where human ears were located and they had small faces that were similar to chimpanzees of earth.

Water reacted different on Emeris due to the lower atmospheric pressure and gravity and also due to the rolling rivers effect of the Moons and both of the Stars that influenced Emeris's orbit.

The water consistency is best explainable in earth terms as the density of approximately six earth atmospheres at earth sea level. It flowed like a thick misty cloud between lands.

The atmosphere pressure above the rivers was much thinner than earths due to slightly lower gravity and faster rotation.

It's seems the atmosphere also rotated easterly with Emeris extending and thinning out into a swirl approximately sixty five kilometers above this unique world.

Wind speeds at surface level were very low due to lower atmosphere pressure and the air circulated with the planets fast rotation.

Each six hour and ten minute day and darkness cycle seemed as tranquil as the garden of Eden must have been in early earth history.

What a marvelous tranquil scene it was.

Esthrep and Crew were able to virtually visit the Emeris population due to a transporter device that allowed the Emerson's to see a projected visual of exactly what the earth humans would look like in their left behind cloned bodies in orbit above Emeris.

The Humans were also able to exist in this holograph projected state even in the Emerson's water cylinder floating rolling dwellings.

Here's a little about the Emerson's biology state on their world.

Yes there were two sexes but different than the male and female species that earthlings would understand.

Their explanation for their sex description was best translated in English as Mela's for the child bearing sex and Melons for the providers.

Not exactly male and female as we know it but more like the mammals or the dolphin species in earth's oceans.

In this society the Melons that are more associated with the male species of earth, bore and birthed the young while the female species was more of the work force and necessity providers.

As far as any government or law controlling bodies, none existed and each clan and its kin lived and respected all other family clans without animosity or strife among any of their species.

The Emerson's had developed scientifically propulsion devices that attached to their bodies and helped them swiftly propel and guide themselves as they swam the light density liquid rivers of Emeris.

They motivated much faster than humans of earth could move under human foot power.

In comparison to earth speeds, they moved in any direction at any given moment at a speed that was estimated to be twenty kilometers per hour.

Instantaneous ninety degree turns in any direction never seemed to bother or effect any of these Emeris beings. Their unique biology was evidently designed to take the full stress of sudden direction change at speeds that would seem very cruel to human beings.

They had to move fast. Their short day and night cycle offered little time for waste. Their version of night sleep was a simple still rest state that reactivated at every red star rise.

After complete hibernated stillness or six hours, they instantly awakened and flashed off in many directions attending the family duties of this multi faceted society.

They had their intellectuals that taught their young in schools. Many fields of study were sought and Emeris science was achieved with due diligence of degrees of masters.

A very keen interest in astronomy was sought but their knowledge of the universes had not reached the level of their present human visitors.

Neither had they at present developed the capability of space travel and atomic propulsion matters.

Although very advanced in some areas, their want to leave their beautiful world had not come to fruition as of yet.

Surely though with new knowledge of the far away Earth visitors, speculation soon stirred among the Emerson's of some day soon developing technology of visiting their planets moons.

As smart and quick learned as the Emerson's were, surely it wouldn't take very many Emeris years for them to achieve that worthy task. Only time and diligence would solve that projected future task.   Not yet had the Emerson's developed satellite technology but learning of the earth concepts from the humans, it seemed inevitable that they soon would.

There was no currency or token need of any sort on this planet and family task and work details were performed specifically for desire and need among families and neighbor.

Once a member of Esthrep's crew caught a family of Emerson's discussing Earth beings and their expression of laughing at their funny appearance.

It was also very amusing to the crew. Visually place a human being beside an Emeris being and the site would tickle anyone's funny bone. That is, indeed if the Emerson's do possessed a comical nature. But we did once hear them laughing at as Earthlings.

This instance of Emerson's laughing at Earth beings also caused laughter among the earth visitors of the Esthrep crew.

Questions of Emeris military status were never discussed because the Emerson's society had no need for a military.

If they indeed had weapons of any nature, it was forbidden to talk of these matters between either species.

All was at peace on Emeris. No clashes of any species was ever a reality here. They the Emerson's, had existed for untold eons as a single peaceful society.

There was an ancient tale of a long ago ice asteroid strike that had once devastated this planet system.

This history was imbedded in all the minds of the Emerson's. They all knew that once Emeris existed in a much different state than it does today. Emeris then, was a much slower rotating world with now extinct land dwelling creatures as huge and as frightening as earths ancient dinosaurs.

As their version describes the legend, Many eons past, a thousand kilometer diameter asteroid split in two pieces upon equatorial approached and struck ancient Emeris just north and south of it's center equatorial rotation in the same direction as the planet spins.

The huge ice asteroid exploded sixty kilometers above the atmosphere then split into and struck Emeris and carved spiral molten rock bottom rivers in both directions towards each pole causing the existing today carved out Emeris river water ways.

The Emeris ice caps at both the north and south pole are the final ice resting place of the existing asteroid remains that occurred on Emeris many eons ago.

That long ago epic event was the final result of the planet Emeris's fast rotation of 12 hours and twenty minutes.

That major event was also the rebirth of Emeris by introducing of much water ice in the form of a mostly ice asteroid that when the molten river rock beds eventually cooled, the water introduced by the comet eventually began to rain soft water that soon filled the rolling rivers and tinted red cloudy skies on planet Emeris.

The Emeris scholars attempted to explain to the humans how much they knew of their own ancient history.

It seems that their technological status at this date in time, let's say we'd compare it to the era of earth history to the early nineteenth century, just past the steam era and into the early petrol engine powered stage.

Esthrep's crew were unanimously careful not to divulge too much information about their Esthrep ship from where they projected their images to the Emerson's through holographic reality.

Also, How they were able to do all of this projecting from each their own chemical orbs safely aboard the Esthrep Probe that brought them to this fascinating star system.

It was decided that each member of the crew would go their own way and visit with and have as many Emeris experiences as possible in their limited orbital visit to this remarkable beautiful planet that existed here in the fantastic solar system around Sirius B.

The Emerson's were somewhat sophisticated in their science but little did they know the potential they had and what their future would entail.

As the Esthrep crew begin to rap up their finale analysis of this Emeris planet, they simultaneously broadcast their goodbyes and good wishes to the many inhabitants that they had visited and shared knowledge. What a fascinating enlightening experience it had been for the entire crew.

The Esthrep Probe and crew silently sailed out of orbit in search of other fascinating treasures that this solar system might have to offer.

Next Destination calculated by the Esthrep crew was a unknown body not too far inward of this world of Emeris.

Engines again roared a mighty thunder as the Esthrep fired its three mighty engines to leave this wonderful new world Emeris that they had just encountered.

Just inward with a mysterious unique orbit that orbited Sirius B in an oblong oval loop. The planets perigee came in close to 170 million kilometers or 105 million miles from the Sirius B star, before being grabbed by Sirius B's gravity and slung back outward again to it's far trailing apogee orbit of 200 million kilometers or 124 million miles before starting its inward journey again of its orbit of Sirius B.

Long range sensors weren't giving explicit details yet but at this distance, there seemed to be a strange vessel of some sort hovering stationary above a tiny moon that chased the yet unknown body in a strange never catching motion that equaled out as a tag along moon but never catching body.

Still too far away the shipped vectored it's thrust towards new awaiting adventure. Destination arrival now computed to be 16 earth hours and 52 minutes.

After the crew's visit with the remarkable Emeris Society, their fluid capacity energy chambers were somewhat depleted from the recent activated encounter.

Esthrep's main computer tracked forward motion and ship's status as the crew recharged in a peaceful stasis state.

Esthrep calculated their recharge time of approximately ten earth hours. Awakening them at that exact time, would be Esthrep's direct faithful task to perform.

Almost silence entailed as the soft clicking of Esthrep's computers recorded the closing distance to their destination ahead.

CHAPTER 20

THE DROGS OF TRIDERIOUS

Twelve hours out now Esthrep began recording more details of the approaching planet now christened Drogus and it's moon named Gouda by the entire Esthrep crew upon awakening.

Though all were in a restful recharge state, they were still sublimely communicating with Esthrep's main computer to record the details as they happened in real time.

Indeed what remarkable earth emissaries they had become.

The crew was always uniquely able to visit these new worlds and the inhabitants in a holographic state, while never leaving the safety of the Esthrep Probe.

Precisely able to be in charged stasis and still maintain their conscious entity existence while pondering of details to come.

The seven were always tied together as one mind to record and assimilate all the fascinating facts of these new worlds and the stars that they orbited.

Rested and recharged now, there was the awakening of the six as Esthrep guided their way to a new destination.

The six simultaneously energized up to their full potential. Each a mind and identity of their own but uniquely tethered electronically together to function as one unit called Esthrep.

Esthrep's Main computer had also recharged itself with the six new awakened entities aboard and was charged challenged and ready. The crew were now awake and linked as one. Esthrep began it's powered down stage as the six crew aboard now controlled their own environment.

Esthrep's long range sensors were still recording several hours out from this new destination. As the Probe got closer, the sensors began revealing more statistics and detailed facts about this new world in the forward view screen for all to assimilate.

Drogus had a diameter of approximately seven thousand kilometers or 4300 miles and glowed in two different colors depending on which star was illuminating it and from which direction that light source came from.

Glowing purplish from the Sirius B's light and yellow from the Sirius A's light, it was a beautiful planet to behold.

Its Ghodi Moon, was rotating fast about once every ten seconds and the continuous reflected pulsating light from A, was as a vision in one's mind of a light house beacon reflecting with precision from a far away shore on a dark sea of earth.

Sensors now detected a rather large satellite that always hovered at a Lagrange point between Drogus and Ghodi.

It was indeed huge and the sensors detected power being sourced from Ghodi and being directed towards a receiving station on the equator of Drogus.

Communications were being searched and the only signal being detected was a microwave signal in the high frequency range.

Esthrep focused it's attention on the detection of intelligent signals now discovered in a high pitch frequency that it was now receiving a signal from.

Onboard translators searched maliciously for a response that could be deciphered or interpreted.

Suddenly Esthrep's computers paused another eureka moment as it had now deciphered the code being used by the inhabitants of this new world Drogus ahead.

The crew projected their greeting as the message was broadcast towards the Planet Drogus.

From Sol we have come from 8.6 light years away in the name of humans from our planet Earth.

This Probe comes peacefully as explorers in hopes to meet other friendly life forms. We six of Esthrep send our regards and hope to make friendly contact with your species. Please reply.

The message languished for the longest moment as silence filled the environment of Esthrep and crew's cabin.

There was static digital crackling as a signal tuned in to the Drogan's confusing response.

The Drogans replied with a firm warning intended to thwart Esthrep's impending approach. Esthrep obeyed the warning and slowed it's speed to almost a hover now of 8,930 miles above Drogus.

Drogus rotated on its axis once every ten hours and eighteen minutes by Earth standards.

On it's white-yellow lit side towards A, distinct metal like structures were detected as the planet rotated towards the darker red glow towards Sirius B, that the Drogus orbited.

Six silent Drogus rotations passed as no further communications was heard from the Drogus inhabitants.

Esthrep and crew still awaited patiently for a reply but none came as expected as the Drogus time continuum passed suspiciously silent in the waiting.

After 130 earth hours, The Drogus inhabitants unexpectedly broadcast a translated voice.

The sound entered the speakers as a static crackle then turned in to a distinguishable tone of a bass nasal voice.

Abruptly, the message turned into a somewhat scrambled video. The viewer displayed a hairy canine dog species with fuzzy whiskered snouts that projected full upon the view screen.

Cautious words of welcome came from the projected emissary now saying these translated words.

We the species that you refer to our planet as Drogus, suspiciously welcome humans of the Sol Earth system but, we are too cautious to allow your visitation at this moment. Our planet's name is Triderious and our species is called Drogs.

I King Revoris speak as the leader of our world. Your patience with our societies reaction to your unexpected arrival will be considered in our reply.

Abruptly again, the communication went silent as almost seven more Triderious rotations occurred.

As 70 hours time passed in awaiting their response, Esthrep and crew gleaned more information from afar about this unique world that they had named Drogus and it's beaconing moon Ghodi.

In the eighth rotation, a direct reply came again across the network of awaited communication and the same long snout entity that spoke before appeared simultaneously on the forward view monitor and spoke these next words.

We Drogs of Triderious, have now arranged a first contact point of reference.

Your ship is to proceed cautiously to an orbit 500 kilometers above Triderious.

Further instructions will be relayed upon inspection of your intentions here towards our species.

Esthrep's engines spat fire that gimbaled towards its rear and Esthrep moved slowly as instructed towards the orbital intentions of King Revoris.

For the first time now, they had a better view of the rosy night side of the planet.

It's gravity measured about forty five percent of earth gravity.

The crew at this point only had a distorted glimpse of a facial view of the King from Triderious.

The rest of his body was yet to be discerned. Hopefully, the Drog race would allow them further details of their existence.

Communications continued as the probe was given a precise location of their first encounter with beings of Triderious.

The Drogs relayed a time of two earth hours to have the earthlings meet the extreme head of defense of their world. Esthrep vectored towards twenty one degrees above the Triderious night sides equator.

Six holographic orbs containing human holographic images now appeared in front of their leader who's name is best translated into English as Revoris. The King is also head governor of the Triderious military council.

Twelve, three meter tall canine like hairy creatures surrounded their arrival as the transporter beam crystallized their projected holographic appearance.

Untranslated growls of caution from the Drogs were murmured as the crew beheld their first view and impressions of the large creatures that now surrounded the five and six feet tall human projections from Earth.

The Drog entities distinctly appeared ten feet tall as four limbed beings with long canine snouts.

They had the ability to walk and move on any two limbs or four when the necessity arrived to do so in a hurry.

Their forward two paw-like limbs had four finger like obtrusions that manipulated computer like devices as they growled their words into the humans translated tongue.

They had tall bodies and wore no humanly clothes but they were uniquely covered with a thick soft fuzzy hair that resembled human hair of earth.

Several had long hair and some others had short hair but all appeared distinct in their appearance.

Spotted reds and blues to yellow black to white to yellow-gold, their specific spotted patches were how they identified each other. No two had the same spots.

When they stood on rear limbs their height measured about three earth meters tall.

Some Drogs were smaller than the others but they were all distinctly discernable by the unique features and spotted colors that they each wore.

Their snouts bore more of a resemblance to a wolf with a fuzzy face.

They had way larger teeth than humans that resembled dog like qualities.

Uniquely, below their long floppy ears, they also had gill like slit appendages under each flap.

They breathed an atmosphere of fifty two percent nitrogen and nearly nineteen percent oxygen with the rest of the percentages being a mixture of helium and hydrogen and argon gasses.

Pressure on surface of this world was about 680 millibars compared to Earth's 1000 millibars pressure at sea level.

Triderious had a lighter gravity of about fifty two percent earth gravity.

These canine like beings moved easily from place to place in leaps. Sometimes, in a hurried distance accomplishment, they moved extremely fast using trots and high skipping bounds in the low gravity.

The twelve Drogus century brigade closed around the earth crew projections as the thirteenth as King began speaking musical low tone growls.

Translated to English the best possible translation came across as follows.

I bid you a cautious welcome as King Revoris of Triderious. My twelve constituents of council and myself wish to know your intentions here are on our planet Triderious

The first statement from crew came across as a cautious question that the Esthrep crew had long practiced for their first response.

We 6 human emissaries of Earth from the Sol system wish to inform you that we are merely mechanical transformed explorers seeking new knowledge of this star system.

Their reply was interrupted with a question of their ship's status in orbit's military capability.

The Triderious leader Revoris loudly demanded complete and immediate divulgence of the humans ship's military capability.

Not wishing to start off on bad intentions the crew detailed a small portion of Esthrep's military might.

They concluded with explaining that their weapons were only for use in case that they were hostilely attacked and they assured the King that they had no intentions of attacking this world or any other that they encountered in their exploration journey.

A pause could have detected a pin drop before Revoris replied in a somewhat cautious but more softer tone.

At this time, We of Triderious are not ready to discuss future contact but we as a united council shall demand that you retreat until further discussions can be held among our distinguished representatives here.

We demand that you remain in your ship until further facts can be assimilated into our worlds computer banks of knowledge.

The King bellowed, Respect our wishes until further details can be ascertained.

The human holographic images immediately disintegrated into thin Triderious air as their holographic similarities returned to the safety of the Esthrep Probe in orbit.

CHAPTER 21
THE DROG ATTACK

Back aboard Esthrep was a time of crew discussions about their first short but exciting meeting with the canine like Drog intelligent inhabitants of Triderious.

Little knowledge had been revealed by the inhabitants except what had been visually ascertained from their first guarded contact with the remarkable inhabitants.

The crew had little knowledge of the Drog's military capabilities but assuredly at present they detected no threat.

Suddenly without warning, Esthrep's defense system fired up and the ship took evasive action to avoid an incoming ballistic device headed for their present position.

Narrowly missing the ship by five meters the device swung around 180 degrees and attempted a second attack on Esthrep.

Esthrep quickly fired it's main engines and again narrowly avoided a second missile attack.

Stunned by the response the ships crew decided to break orbit and obtain a more distant point away from the Drog's planet.

The missile fell silently back towards Triderious. For a few scarce moments they now had their doubts about these strange creatures they had encountered only hours earlier.

The crew murmured frantically amongst themselves in shock of what had just occurred. Not knowing the Drog's military capabilities, they chose to not respond immediately unless they were attacked again.

Long silent moments slowly passed as they awaited further response from the aliens of this world. Now a safer distance away, their defense mechanism remained on high alert as they awaited the possibility of another unwanted attack.

More long hours passed as no further attacks came. In due time, a message response finally arrived from the Drog's King Revoris.

The message now translated read as follows.

We of Triderious have directed our missile at your ship to test your resolve and to ascertain if you would respond in a war like manner.

The missile was deliberately programmed to only pass close to your ship and not cause harm to you.

However, we do have the ability to destroy your ship and if you had responded with weapons, we surely would have done so.

Since you chose to not attack in response, I King Revoris of Triderious, have decided that you are truly peaceful creatures that mean us no real harm.

Our council has decided to welcome you again as visitors from your Sol System and extend our highest regards in hopes of future contact.

In several of your earth time periods, we will extend further details of our next meeting. Best regards from King Revoris.

Several Earth day periods passed with no further communication from the Drog's planet. The Esthrep Probe remained a safe distance away from the Drog inhabited world that had recently tested their willingness to wage a war against an unknown adversary.

Time passed ever so slowly awaiting further contact from the curious response they had received from the Drog King.

Although canine like in appearance and warlike in ways, their first contact had led the Earth crew to believe that there was still hope for a peaceful contact with the alien species of Triderious.

Esthrep's main computers were continuously assimilating data on the planet and it's moons.

It had ascertained that Triderious was approximately 4,100 miles or 6600 kilometers in diameter and rotated once approximately every sixteen Earth hours.

The closest orbiting Moon named Percivus was in a revolving orbit that went around the planet every 5 and a half Earth days. Percivus orbital perigee was approximately five thousand kilometers or 3106 thousand miles above Triderious and the moon's apogee went out to 5,000 miles or 8,000 kilometers in its orbit around the planet.

Triderious orbit was influenced by both stars. When the planet was between A and B in its orbit, Its orbit apogee was influenced by Sirius A.

Triderious was lit brightly on one side by Sirius A and shadowy lit by its host star Sirius B.

Its close Moon Percivus which simultaneous lit the dimmer side in different shades depending on where the moon was in it's orbit.

Such a grand system of worlds that it's hard to describe the beauty in earth known terms.

Human from Earth would have been so inspired by the beauty of these worlds that orbited around two stars like this crew was observing and recording through their main computer screen.

Triderious also had a smaller asteroid size moon named Palous that orbited far away very slowly at a distance of about 580 thousand kilometers or 360,395 miles and was only about twenty five kilometers in diameter.

It's pale light was very insignificant to the total shading light of the closer larger moon named Percivus. All in all, it was indeed such a remarkable set of heavenly bodies to behold.

More Earth periods elapsed and after about eighteen Earth periods, Esthrep's computers finally received a decoded message from the Drog world below.

The message began with a warning for the crew to submit to their worlds inspection of Esthrep's military capability and if those conditions were agreed upon they the Drog King Revoris would then consider a second peaceful meeting of the Drog inhabitants.

Esthrep's crew immediately went into combined conference over the distressing message received from the Drog inhabitants.

For certain, they were not willing to submit to such unreasonable demands to inspect their ships military defense or offense capability.

Esthrep was not willing to give up a contact opportunity so easily. Long conferences were held among the crew to discern their response to the Drogs.

Finally there was agreed to a response that they the Esthrep crew deemed appropriate to send to the Drogs.

In response they prepared the message as follows.

This Probe and crew are from the star system Sol and planet Earth. We intend not to offend or harm any on your world.

Although we respectfully decline inspection of our offense and defense capability, we assure you King Revoris of Triderious and your governing council, that we are here only on an exploration and peaceful contact mission.

We are somewhat offended by your missile attack but we do understand your reason for doing so.

If only there is someway that we two different species can agree to meet peacefully under guarded circumstances.

We humans of Earth from the Sol system will be willing to accommodate you Drogs in any way possible other than divulging or military capability.

We assure you again that we mean no harm to any on your world but we would like very much to meet again under better circumstances.

If you of Triderious decide that this is not satisfactory, then this exploration Probe from Earth, will leave your solar system and explore other peaceful contact possibilities elsewhere.

Best regards from the crew of Esthrep. We the crew of Esthrep respectfully await your finale reply with hopeful ambitions.

CHAPTER 22
THE FURRY OF DROGS

Many more earth hours passed and as of yet no reply was received from the Drog inhabitants

Meanwhile, Esthrep's computers searched the system to see if any satellites or any means of space vehicles were detected.

None were detected and the crew assumed that their military capability was at the point of early twenty century Earth technology. But to assume anything at this point in this time continuum, could certainly be a grave mistake for the Esthrep crew to make at this point in negotiations.

Discussions were held among the crew as to the next steps to be taken in hopes of any further contact from the Drog world.

It was decided that if the Drogs didn't reply in one more Earth week's time, that the probe's crew would abandon hopes of contact and move onward in their exploration journey.

At the end of three earth days, they received a reply from King Revoris as follows.

I King Revoris of Triderious and my Council, have considered your proposal and have come to the conclusion that it would be in both of our interest to have a second contact meeting with humans from Earth.

In twenty four of your Earth hour periods, I recommend a meeting near the same location that we have supplied earlier. The message ended with the co ordinance and went silent.

The crew was excited that they would have a second chance of meeting with the Drogs of Triderious.

For the next twenty four hours they made preparations. The crew got ready for hopefully a peaceful meeting with these Drog inhabitants of Triderious.

Surely the probe and crew had misgivings of a Trojan horse scenario. Any attempt to take over Esthrep, had been strategized and programmed into Esthrep's defense.

Since they were going as holographic images, they had little doubt that if any deception were detected, that Esthrep's Main computers could easily whisk them back to the probe in an instant if it became necessary.

Evidently the Drogs didn't realize yet that their images were merely holographs and possibly their technology had not developed to the point of projecting holographic images yet.

The time arrived for the meeting of beings from two separate star systems.

Esthrep's computers energized the holographs to the co ordinance and as quickly as a whisper in time, they appeared this time in front of a giant room of a hundred or more Drog creatures.

Many growls of Drog murmurs filled the grand auditorium as the Earthling holographs first appeared in front of many Drog eyes.

Several long Earth moments passed as the chatter continued and gradually slowed to a softer more receptive tone.

At the head of a staged podium, there stood on two of its four limbs the head council and King of the Triderious planet.

The crowds growling murmurs died down as King Revoris began to address the Esthrep crew as their translator began to formulate and translate the King's barking words.

Although originally, the head rulers words sounded like growling barking sounds, the words soon formulated into softer human language sounds and the first response came across as follows.

We of this Drog species call ourselves Drogs that dwell here on this planet that you have wrongly referred to as Drogus in your peculiar language.

In our language this planet is entitled Triderious. And We are Drogs.

As King and head of this council and ruler over all Triderious, I King Revoris wish to inform you humans of Earth, that we are very cautious in dealing with alien species due to a destructive warring past with other species.

We tested your response with an attack in our immediate space to see if you were a hostile alien species.

Your non offensive response was very much appreciated and welcomed by our society here on Triderious.

Although the missiles you encountered were only determined to test your response to an attack from our world, Let me assure you earthlings that if we had intended to destroy your probe, We Drogs of Triderious are certainly capable of doing so.

The mechanical voice translation now assumed a much more reasonable friendly tone as the computer mechanism became finely tuned to the growls of the head rulers barking voice.

Here among many Drogs, the rustling growls of the many others, grew softly to whispers as the Drogs now patiently awaited the response from the six, two meter, simulated holographic, human peculiar images that stood projected upon a pedestal before the head council King.

Each Earthling spoke numerically in their agreed order one at a time but 5 and 6 never got to ask questions before the King got angry and expelled the crew.

1 = Yes our ship that we call Esthrep is equipped with weapons. We emphatically must assure you that those weapons are for self defense in any emergency that could have occurred on our 20 earth year journey to this Sirius system.

2 = We six, are a projection representation only of a human species from the Sol system of eight major planets.

As far as we humans presently know, the only planet in our solar system that supports intelligent life, is our home planet Earth that is the third world away from our Sun.

Our DNA life presence, exist only in the ceramic Orbs aboard the Probe Esthrep in orbit.

3 = We as human projected holograms, are incapable of physically harming anything while in this projected state in your presence.

Living human beings themselves, are incapable of making long space voyages such as the one here to visit your species of Drogs.

We hope that you truly understand that we are a peaceful species and are only here to explore and meet intelligent species such as yourself.

4 = We are here to harm no beings of your beautiful planet. Of that you can be assured. We are very pleased to make your acquaintance and hope that you feel the same way.

There was a short pause as the murmurs of the many Drog sounds began again and eventually died down enough to hear the head rulers response to the six holographic human projections standing before the head council.

The head council King Revoris of Triderious interrupted their speech.

We Drogs retired our space explorations aspirations many of your earth centuries ago.

Long ago, we traversed the expansion of space and our ancient records record that we did indeed visit your planet Earth. That occurred well over twenty five thousand of your Earth years ago.

The human species of those long ago days were a primitive frail species living among huge dinosaur creatures in a struggle for daily survival.

Planet Earth was drastically evolving in your Sol system in those days and at the very end of a warm hot climate, Your Star soon entered into a dormant low sol state and it's output dropped to approximately 70 percent of it's normal luminosity.

It was becoming very cold on Earth before the time of our departure.

We Drogs taught the primitives of Earth how to build huge pyramid structures and the secret of how to move larger boulders with the secret white powder that we furnished certain individuals.

Before departure, Our Ancestors of Triderious, worked with ancient humans on earth of that ancient day. We taught the ancient humans of the dessert lands how to build large pyramid survival shelters.

The secret milky white powder was the key as to how huge stones were easily moved?

The Triderious scientist of our ancient earth visit decided to crossbreed a lower dna version of ourselves with a wolf being among your animal species in order to give the animal the knowledge to survive the projected coming cold state of your future planets evolution.

We are now curious as to if that lower version of our being has survived and prospered among your planet's animal species.

The Earthlings were intrigued by this curious question.

Why yes indeed they responded one. The animal species that you have referred to are called dogs by humans and have become a very important friend and companion to many humans on our home world.

In fact, that have become very important to many humans with many disabilities and their capabilities have been very helpful to our police and fire fighting emergency responders.

The Dogs of earth are indeed very intelligent creatures.

The head rulers snout sniffed upwardly in the Triderious atmosphere, as a determined gesture of appreciation of the news of dogs of Earth's existence.

It did seem at that moment that The King's audience was very pleased also of the news and expressed it in three second bouts of growl sniffing. The audience of Drogs all expressed some appreciation in a similar manner.

So it seemed now to the earthlings that dogs existed through the long cold spell of Earths frozen past even when the huge dinosaurs were unable to survive the cataclysm bombardment of a frozen large ice asteroid impacts of long ago Earth history.

Earthlings too were excited of the news that dogs had been placed among earth animal species from a long ago visit from these Drogs of Triderious.

CHAPTER 23
ΠΕUΕR SAY CAT TO A ΚΙΠG

The conversation now progressed back and forth between the two species as the number four human asked a question to the head Drog entitled King Revoris

Of the Dogs of our world ,there is also a curious species called cats and it has always been a wonder as to why dogs are so hostile to cats?

King Revoris snarled, spit, barked and jumped high in the low gravity then barked again in their projected faces as he landed directly in front of the six holograph projections.

The King upon landing was very angry at the gall of the statement and the surrounding Drog audience became very agitated also .

The King pounced high again and landed this time even more hostile and viciously growled vocally at the humans words.

The translation came.

So you are a spy probe that has been sent here by the Cratt's of Sirius A.

His angry response continued for a long Triderious time span as King Revoris growled angrily while hop pacing. He was obviously even more irritated at the mention of cats that he instantly associated the cat word spoken with the Cratt Society that the Drogs were at war with.

He pounced high for a third time and angrily ordered the Earth beings to immediately depart back to their ship until further notice.

The Earthlings knew nothing of the Cratt Society and weren't given any opportunity to reply or ask further questions.

They were surprised at The King's sudden angered outburst and immediately signaled Esthrep Main in orbit to energized their holographs back to the safety of the Esthrep Probe.

Several Earth rotation periods passed with no further response or communication from the Drogs of Triderious.

The silence aboard Esthrep was unanticipated and a sudden fear awareness became prevalent among the crew.

No one really knew what to expect next and the Esthrep Probe had now regressed into a higher orbit above the Drog world.

Discussions were occurring among the entire crew about what had been learned so far about these mysterious intelligent three meter tall canine like beings that inhabited all of Triderious.

It was duly noted that although similar in appearance to Canine creatures of Earth, many of these creatures although they did have four limbs, often moved around from place to place on only their lower legs in a bounding spring like kangaroo hop.

This hop movement was due to the lighter gravity that Drog's endured on their home Planet Triderious and their inner ear balance was amazing.

At Times when traveling a great distance, they ran on all four limbs and obtained high speed in long leaped hop maneuvers.

Five more Earth twenty four hour periods passed before a message finally came from the Drogs of Triderious in a somewhat curious format.

They themselves were now requesting information about the cat species of present day Earth.

It appeared that they wanted more information on how cats reacted to a dogs presence in a close quarter situation on our world.

This was very curious to the Esthrep crew because although dogs and cats were somewhat natural enemies on earth, they were not considered to be intelligent species like the Drogs of Triderious.

It seemed to the crew, that something was missing in their curious question about the cat species of Earth.

This time it was the Esthrep crew who gave a silent response for a few Earth periods.

Not knowing exactly how to respond to their cat curiosity, the crew finally responded with the truth that cats and dogs of Earth had always been natural enemies to each other from the earliest recorded history.

They also made it very clear that in many homes, dogs and cats have been trained to now live together and get along well.

This latest response message from Esthrep and crew seemed to make the Drogs more at ease and suddenly the crew were invited back to a third conference among the Drog population.

CHAPTER 24
THIRD DROG ENCOUNTER.

Cautiously the Esthrep human holographs energized and appeared again before the Drog leader and his audience of many other Drogs.

More growls and murmurs again eventually died down as the head council ruler bounced to a forward podium and began to speak in low barks and growls to the humans.

His words soon became translated and the Earthlings were now being informed of a long ago past lethal war between the Cratt population from the inner bright Sirius A star system that they called the Cratt Star.

Of course, Earthlings had always referred to the brightest star as Sirius A but that was beside the point because the Earthlings were the real aliens here in this three star system of suns.

In the habitual zone of the Cratt Sirius A star, there exist a planet that they the Drogs called Crattius.

Deep hatred memories of a long ago attempted communication with this Cratt world, had caused the very beginning a lethal chemical war between their Drog species and the Cratts.

Revoris went on to say that, a violent long time war has endured and still exist until this very day.

It was explained that the two species had absolutely total disdain for each other.

In fact, in only a few Triderious solar periods before the Esthrep crew arrived, an all out furious space battle occurred with both side losing many lives.

It was originally thought by the Drogs that the Esthrep Probe was a sneaky attempt of the Cratts to attack their planet again like they had many times before.

It was duly noted the Drogs considered the Cratt population to be very sneaky and deceptive creatures that deserved no respect from any Drog inhabitants.

The war between close star worlds, had continued for many eons and until this very time continuum period, it still does.

Now, lets set the Esthrep recorded facts straight.

The Drogs of this world resembled the canine species of earth but there are very distinct unique differences. First, they are large compared to humans in height.

Second, Drogs on Triderious are very intelligent even more so than the humans realized.

There were many species of Drogs just like there are many species of dogs on earth. Drogs here lived on a light gravity planet and mostly manipulated their motion on their considered hind legs and in soft bounding strides.

Their jointed upper five feet long limbs and paws, were used much as humans used their arms hands and fingers. Their upper arm movements were extremely fast and precise.

They had four extended fingers on their upper limbs with short scarped nails that were very useful in picking up and moving objects around.

Their paw nails appeared slightly extended but sharp as needles on the fingers of their webbed hands. The Drogs manipulative objects with ease between individuals.

Instead of human faces, there were some of the smaller one meter tall Drogs that had very unique Qula bear faces. For unknown reasons, most of the short Drog species had very short ears also with scales below their flaps.

The Drogs were definitely of the canine species but like the record explains, they the Drogs had their own unique differences from the canine species of earth.

The King had a two foot long goiter beard below his snouted teethed mouth.

Drog's technological society had long ago developed into a space faring and scientific developed planet.

They the Drogs and Cratts were equal in intelligence and technology.

In fact, in several ways, they were indeed more intelligent than humans are.

That fact is evident in their past technology of their long ago visit to Earth, before it went into its long ago frozen dinosaur destroyer period.

These newly revealed details answered many questions to the Esthrep crew about ancient Earth's unknown history.

Details seemed to make much more sense as to why they were initially treated in such a distrustful manner upon arrival here above this Triderious Drog planet.

For the first time, the Drog head ruler Revoris spoke in a more trustful and even tone to the humans standing before the audience of many Drogs.

Now, The King believed that the probe was truly from the sol world over eight point six light years distance away. The King no longer thought the humans were a sneaky attempt from the Cratt star world as the Drogs had originally suspected.

The King then revealed to the crew, when his ancestors visited Earth many eons ago, they had mixed molecule portions of their DNA with the then wolf species of earth in hopes that some day that they would return and find canine beings like themselves.

Although dogs of earth are highly intelligent and considered humans best friends, dogs of earth couldn't compete with the intelligence of the Drogs of Triderious.

Esthrep was very intrigued by all of this new information but the crew were very cautious about asking about the Cratt society

Bravely, number 5 did get a chance to timidly ask if the King thought that the Cratt's would attack the Esthrep Probe if they were to journey to the Cratt Planet.

The Drog ruler sarcastically replied. You must understand that the Cratt's are highly sophisticated.

Many eon's ago, their society also visited Earth at the same time period that we Drogs were there.

In fact, they started a war with us way back then above that planet that you call Mars.

That war in your solar system, nearly destroyed the then Martian water world that it once was.

At that time, both of our species were highly sophisticated in technology while the then humans like your earth ancestors, were scarcely populated and living as cave dwellers. At the time, neither species expected the humans to ever survive but we tried to help a few.

We Drogs can see now that humans have developed into a intelligent space faring society. Although we don't quite understand the nature of your holographic state. I King Revoris do recognize now that you are indeed very intelligent beings from the Sol system and planet Earth.

Our ancient war mostly bypassed your Earth. The war nearly destroyed planet Venus in an all out attempt to destroy each other.

It was a vicious war with the Cratts in those days long ago in your solar system.

It was our atomic and lethal chemical weapons that caused a cataclysmic chain reaction that stopped Planet Venus's eastward rotation and filled its atmosphere with toxic poisonous fumes from our then chemical weapons arsenal.

Both warring parties manufactured our chemical weapons from the then Venus surface material and by the time the war in that area was all over, we had caused a chain greenhouse effect on the then second world you call Venus.

Many Atomic bombs dropped by both species, had caused the planet to reverse its poles and spin slowly opposite from the other planets of your system.

Our other atomic weapons that you call nuclear weapons, caused the planet to temporality stop rotating and reverse its poles as it turned upside down and started rotating very slowly westward.

In those days, temperatures on Venus were increasing very rapidly and by the time we Drogs and Cratt's had returned to our home worlds, Venus remained uninhabitable forever.

Above your planet Mars was the final battle in your Sol system and we also did much damage to that planet.

Before the wars of those days were over. Mars once was in the early development stage and was beginning to sustain primordial plants and animal life.

Our war with the Cratt's, caused much damage to your Sol system and for this catastrophe, We the Drogs are truly regretful of those occurrences.

You must understand that we Drogs of that time period, had very little evidence that humans even existed on your world.

We only knew then of mostly the huge dinosaur creatures that roamed the lands of your planet.

We did know then of the few humans of that time but both societies considered them inferior as non threatening intelligent animal creatures that had very little future in the development of your Earth.

The King continued his statements.

We do understand that apologies now mean very little but warring times of those days were very hostile and even followed both societies into their exploration days of your own solar system.

The translation to English came behind a more docile canine whinnying sound from the rulers snout. He had a much more friendly tone towards the human explorers. In fact the entire canine audience now had a friendlier reception tone towards the humans.

The more relaxed Esthrep crew member 6, was brave enough to ask the head ruler more information about the Cratt world and what would possibly be their reception from the Cratt's if they decided to visit their world. She asked further, what would possibly be the repercussions if they did?

The Drog ruler immediately growled at the question and became angry again warning the humans that if they were fool enough to try such an exploration, that the Cratt's would surely consider them a threat and possibly destroy them and their Esthrep Probe.

He continued, You Earthlings have no idea how ruthless and sneaky that the Cratt's can be.

Their technology is as advance as ours and they certainly would not like humans interfering in our warring affairs. Especially if they knew that you had visited Triderious first.

Number 6 replied, well surely with your permission, we could attempt to communicate and be an unbiased peaceful ambassador. Possibly we humans could even set up an armistice agreement or truce between both of your worlds. What would it hurt to try?

Angrily Revoris replied, You would be totally destroyed Revoris growled. Those Cratts are a hateful deceitful society and their way of life is nothing like you have observed here on our Triderious planet.

Surely you would be ignorant fools to even try such a thing.

Even though this hate war has survived for many of you centuries, they have no interest in making peace.

In fact, they actually love the hate that they have for us Drogs and our world.

Like I stated before, Cratt's are very sneaky and you can't trust anything that they say or do.

They have no need to consider peace and neither do we Drogs. We have always been enemies and as far as I King Revoris am concerned, we always will be enemies.

The humans were left with a conundrum of how to get the Drogs to consider an armistice approach and the possibility of letting them the humans try to talk to the Cratt's on their behalf.

The Drog ruler would have no part of this suggestion and quickly dismissed the possibility.

However, they the humans were invited to visit the Triderious society outside the enclosed auditorium that they now stood in the presence of many Drogs.

CHAPTER 25
THE DROG SOPHISTICATED SOCIETY.

The Drogs of Triderious were both male and female and raised their families in complicated structured houses and cities. At least they didn't refer to their dwellings as homes like we do on earth but the translation came down to a word like bungalows.

They had streets laid out in geometrical patterns much like block cities of earth but their dwellings appeared larger than normal earth dwellings. Many of the bungalows were circular in their dimensions and only a few had more than one story.

Windows as we know them were not visible anywhere on the bungalows but it was explained that they had the ability to look through the walls due to a technology that the earthlings couldn't yet explain.

What was surprising is that through the spectrum of ROYGBIV colors, their were so many unexplainable shades and colors of the bungalows that none matched any other in colors.

They used vehicles to transport along their mostly straight roadways and the vehicles were nothing like a human could imagined. Certainly not like anything that they had ever knew about on earth.

Transports had no wheels and seem to float and levitate a half meter above their wide reflecting roadway surface.

Their roadways had pole reversing magnetically charged magnets under the surface that formed an invisible U shaped magnetic repulsion tunnel along the roadways to the magnets on the bottom of their vehicles.

Vehicles were shaped more like two revolving infused angled floating pyramids, they were surly a sight to behold as they rotated silently along not producing any noise or pollution.

There were also large air transport vehicles that hovered like earth helicopters at times. Several air ships moved swiftly off into various directions at silent but fast speeds.

Some of these air ships were quite large and seemed to morph into more streamlined shapes as they zoomed across the sky in many directions.

The land flora was quite different than anything on earth in ways that are quite impossible to describe fully in words.

Far out of the cities where there were no dwellings, in the fields along side the roadways you could see many unique plants and trees. Trees here grew much higher and larger than trees of Earth.

It was surmised that that was possibly due to a lighter gravity planet and rich underground water streams below the surface.

Where there were grasses, they weren't green like the grasses of earth but many had a purplish rosy tint to their flowered tops that were kept nicely trimmed by Drog farmer trimming machine mechanisms.

There were flying fouls here but unlike earth birds, they had much wider wing spans and none had beaks but instead they had tiny snouts that animated their mostly bald heads.

Esthrep also surmised that the large wing spans were due to a lighter gravity and thinner atmosphere than earth has.

With our translators we were able to converse with many Drog families and gain quite a bit of Drog characteristics of how they lived worked and survived here on this alien world to humans.

Of course the crew of Esthrep were the real aliens here on Triderious and physics as we knew it were somewhat different here.

There came a time that passed that we the Esthrep crew felt that we were over staying our welcome here and decided to plead one more time to the head council ruler about the possibility of contacting the

Cratts about an armistice and some sort of peace agreement between the Drogs and the Cratts.

Again we were warned about voyaging to the Cratt world and were told that we should stay out of this and mind our own human business by the head council King Revoris of Triderious.

The short days of Triderious passed quickly now and the nighttime sky was lit by Triderious moons. The day sky was lit by two stars with the closest star B giving most of the planet its needed heat.

Sirius A in the distance, furnish it's brighter yellow light.

Although Sirius A was way larger, it was much further away than their life giving star Sirius B the earth sized rosy white dwarf.

Never able to reach an agreement of peace with the head council, the Esthrep crew were now returned to their ship and in conference with each other about what steps to take now and how they would proceed in the immediate future.

CHAPTER 26
DESTINATION CRATTIUS

It all started out immediately after they had said all of their farewells and all of their final goodbyes and gave their deep gratifications and thanks for all of the new facts and experiences that they had learned while visiting Triderious.

In a twinkle sparkling instant, the Esthrep six were energized back to the ceramic amino acid globe chambers safely aboard Esthrep in orbit above Triderious.

The six were seven again and six of the seven now slept in order to recharge and download all of the new learned Drog and Cratt knowledge that they had assimilated upon their Triderious explorations.

The decision was made to go to the Cratt system before the crew retired.

Esthrep Main functioned alone and had calculated that the Journey to Cratt in the inner Sirius A star system would take just over 39 earth days.

The crew regenerated for nine days and that regeneration could in no way be interrupted.

Esthrep alone wasn't allowed to interrupt that regeneration under any circumstances.

Thirty days to Cratt and Esthrep sailed alone. The safety of the Probe was the entire responsibility of Esthrep the main computer entity.

The ship had sailed gently away from Triderious.

To conserve fuel, it used the gravity of the Triderious moon to slingshot and leave the system.

Day ten was when it all began and Esthrep was to be tested unexpectedly twenty six hours after the crew had entered recharge and download sleep.

Sudden silence was interrupted as Esthrep was violently awakened by a loud banging vibration just outside the port next to where Esthrep's Main Orb chamber core existed.

Bang ! Bang ! It sounded louder this time.

It appeared that something physical was banging a fist on the hull just outside the probe hull very close to where Esthrep Main was.

Six meters away it was if something was banging on the metal hull door for the emergency robotic repair and defense drones.

Louder this time ! The bang sound echoed through Esthrep's Orb.

Something was causing it. Just outside the hull door, something was causing that disruption to Esthrep's now interrupted journey.

Esthrep had detected no breach of its defenses.

Yet something was knocking against the hull .

Three defense probes were immediately dispatched from the opposite starboard side of Esthrep and the escape hatch door.

Suddenly with a loud metal ripping scrape, the door was forced open by physical might. Air pressure hissed out as the door was bent and hanging on to the side of the exposed to space extremely cold vacuum.

Outside the door and hanging on to the side of Esthrep, there was a mean looking ugly alien Cratt.

It hung on and was four meters tall with large muscles and knobby joints. The Cratt was unimaginably huge.

This Feline Cratt was nearly four meters tall with mustard yellow fire colored fur and it also had fleshy huge arm claw muscles that would be beyond human comprehension.

Esthrep's three floating repair probes were immediately destroyed by the creature that quickly grabbed them one by one and sailed them smashing to bits against the inner hull door.

The creature just stood there at first still pounding the remaining door frame it had torn off a few minutes before.

Sound wasn't transmitted now because the main cabin module had been decompressed from what little inside pressure that Esthrep required.

It bent its body and stepped in. The Cratt stood bent over for another minute glaring it's ugly eyes toward Esthrep' main console command chamber orb.

The Cratt's nose had huge meter long whiskers that slimmed a acid liquid from its nostrils that steamed the metal walls as the slime made contact. The acid was a chemical version of their space suit protection system.

Just inside the hull door the creature hung by its claw toes while bending over in the three meter tall ceiling inside Esthrep.

Esthrep now detected that there was a huge metal black cube ship that Esthrep's sensors had been unable to detect earlier.

Just inside the torn door hatch hung an ugly alien huge muscled furry catlike creature with claws like eagles jutting from two of its muscular pawed fist.

The creature was snarling acid from its nostril inside the hull and it didn't advance any further than the inner doorway.

Outside the door sailed a huge black twenty meters in diameter bumpy block black ship.

The ship silently hovered alongside Esthrep in its journey to the now thirty one days away from the Cratt Planet.

The huge ugly creature just hung there weightless looking angry and snarling towards Esthrep's five meter diameter crystal chamber that housed the main essence and existence of Esthrep the leader of the probe.

Suddenly after an invasive intrusion, the creature snarled and turn and sprang fifty meters from the bent doorway across the emptiness of black space to a huge doorway on the side of the black dark ship.

It floated across and grabbed a rail along side it's black ship hatch and quickly opened a door and disappeared inside.

The Cratt intrusion was over and the black ship suddenly disappeared. Esthrep rightly comprehended and assimilated that the probe had just been introduced to the Cratts for the first time while Esthrep sailed the void alone.

Esthrep reviewed the recorded excursion on the monitor several times.

So quickly from departure of the Triderious vicinity, the Cratts had discovered the earth probe and seemed to dismiss it as if it was only s non threatening communication satellite beacon of some sort.

The Cratts eleven feet tall alien had torn the door off and stepped viciously near Esthrep's main computer crystal ball acid filled five meter diameter core while inspecting the inner probe visually for the longest time and evidently considered the probe not to be a threat to the inner Sirius A Cratt planet.

The recordings revealed that after looking around without advancing, the ugly alien catlike creature suddenly turned and leaped spaceward floating gracefully for thirty seconds then grabbed a rail next to the ships hatch door as it swiftly pawed a touch mechanism and the hatch opened silently and it disappeared quickly behind a closing hatch now back on board its own ship

The ship then proceeded back to the business of monitoring the Triderious Drog world.

It existed now not too far away while hiding in a dark stealth ship built for spying.

Any human would have been frightened.

Esthrep was not human. Esthrep was a super computer probe leader and captain of this probe with the responsibility of guarding six others who recharged astern under Esthrep's care.

Immediately Esthrep dispatched three more robotic repair probes that began repairing the door that the Cratt alien had easily ripped open with little effort at all.

Esthrep mentally regained its composure and frantically digressed into a three day repair attempt.

It's recorded Cratt encounter would be played to the sleeping six when their recharge cycle was complete.

But for now, Esthrep sailed onward towards Cratt only two weeks out from the Triderious worlds that they left behind.

On day twelve the hatch door repairs were efficiently completed and now Esthrep guided the probe and crew silently ahead. It anxiously anticipating the awakening of the crew in a week.

The next week was mostly uneventful except for a pressure leak that had to be repaired due to the still leaking rubber seal around the recently repaired hatch door.

All said and done, Esthrep now used its three remaining repair probes and repaired itself and again was fully operable and able to continue its journey.

Time quickly passed and the awakening process dutifully began and in a single hours time, the crew would be fully awake and be immediately informed of Esthrep's lone Cratt encounter while they were in recharge mode.

Seven days out the crew were awakened and all were totally informed of the Cratt encounter.

Esthrep now required a two day recharge mode itself and the second in command now guided them all while Esthrep the main command began its own recharge to regain its full potential.

All had proceeded well for the next couple of days as Esthrep and crew sailed closer to the edge of this Cratt star's Sirius A system.

Esthrep had detected far ahead a planet that appeared to be in the habitable zone of the hotter than normal star but details were not clear now that they were a week away from their destination Planet Cratt.

There were also three jovian type gas worlds in this solar system but Esthrep's intended destination was a planet just inside the stars goldilocks habitable zone.

It was considered to be what the Drogs referred to as Crattius the Drogs long time enemy planet.

CHAPTER 27
ANOTHER INTRUSION

Two days out from Cratt there suddenly without warning appeared beside Esthrep another dark large cubical ship.

The dark alien Cratt ship was ten times larger than the Esthrep probe and was 5 kilometers in diameter.

Immediately upon arrival out jutted a huge mechanical grappling claw and latched onto the Esthrep probe's nose ring hook at the front of the probe. Esthrep's motion now was under the control of the Cratt ship's complete control.

This time no alien ripped the door off. Esthrep had been stopped in its forward journey and prevented further inward travel.

For six earth hours, there was no contact what so ever made between ships and the dark black ship just continually held the probe in its mechanical claw and prevented further excursion.

In those hours Esthrep could detect a deep scan being done to the main memory banks. Esthrep had immediately shut down the crew to prevent them from being detected by the invasive deep unwanted probe.

The main computer control module was equipped with an emergency cloaking device to shield the crew in case an incident like this occurred.

Deep inside Esthrep's main computer core it could detect the alien probe trying to defeat the cloaking mechanism that insured the crews survival and kept them safe.

Esthrep's computer code eventually won the battle and after many deep probe hours the alien probe had given up and determined that the Esthrep probe was no threat to the Cratt planet that was a few earth days travel away.

As suddenly as it had began the claw grip was released by the Cratt ship and their inward destination to the Cratt planet was silently resumed again.

One day later the Esthrep main computer assumed that the danger had passed and the six in stasis were again revived and shared the experience that the main computer experienced in their sleep.

Esthrep after handing command to another resumed his recharge mode that had been recently interrupted by the large Cratt defense probe.

These Cratt ships were automated guards of the Cratrs to defend them from unwanted intruders to their planet.

Placed way out here on the deep edge of their inward solar system, the Cratts had engineered a defensive protector from the Drogs of Triderious.

Very ingenious indeed but not to preclude the fact that the Drogs also had their own ingenious defense squadron called Shadowdrogs in the far out vicinity of their own planets orbit.

The Shadowdrogs were known to also zero in on passing ships in their system.

Two days out from Crattius, Esthrep was confronted this time by several alien shadow crafts and all of it's computer commands immediately went into a stress mode and the crew again were protected by Esthrep computer command module that was hidden and attached to the very front nose of the Esthrep probe.

Esthrep again was in a survival mode.

The crew now hidden from detection, Esthrep began scanning one of the shadow vessels   that had again captured it. This time it was the Drogs.

Another Intrusion

Several hours had passed and suddenly a Drog video appeared to Esthrep command screen demanding an inspection of it's intentions in this far out space quadrant.

Esthrep complied to an extent and insinuated that the recent visit to Triderious would explain their cause and intensions.

In twenty minutes time their explanation had been satisfactory to the Shadowdrogs that defended the outer boundaries of their planet here in the vacuum distance between the Drog world and the Cratt world.

Lethal enemies for eons. That mostly defines what is the attitudes from both societies thus far.

Still, the real Cratts hadn't met the crew of the Esthrep probe yet either. Again the Esthrep probe was discerned as non threatening and released to continue its voyage.

A days travel left and the inward bound Esthrep probe continued its voyage after being released by the Shadowdrogs defense probes.

The crew again were revived to the present status and informed of the recent encounters with the Drog Ships.

There was much concern on whether this probe would be able to survive another alien encounter. But most felt that it was essential that they proceed with the best intentions from earth.

The entire Esthrep probe agreed that the best plan lay dead ahead in the forward destination of the Crattius Planet.

The Planet Crattius orbited it's host star at a distance of approximately two hundred and fifty million earth miles or 402 million kilometers.

Sirius A was almost twice the diameter of Earth's sun and the habitable zone was right in the middle of where the Crattius Planet orbited.

For the first time now the Esthrep's probe was able to see the Crattius world in the viewer screen.

CHAPTER 28
WELCOME TO CRATTIUS

Purple yellow in color, the rotating world loomed in the viewer.

Wispy white and gray clouds trailed the swirled colors in the opposite direction of planet Cratt's fast spin.

Slightly larger than the diameter of Earth's Moon, this spinning marble planet had very unique orbital properties.

It's orbital distance from Sirius A ranged from a perigee of two hundred and fifty million miles in to an oblong orbit that slings the planet outward to three hundred eighty million miles at its furthest outward orbit in its apogee.

It's yearly revolve around Sirius A takes well over five earth solar years time.

The Planet Crattius was a mere two thousand four hundred miles in diameter.

A planet with extremely dense compaction and its gravity way stronger than anyone could possibly have expected by earth known physics.

Compared with the five point five earth compaction model of earth's average ground surface,

Esthrep detected that the surface compaction of Cratt was at least ten times earth ground compaction measurements.

In fact, the entire small planet was super compressed matter to the point that in had more than three times the gravity on the surface than planet earth does.

The Esthrep Probe's mass was 3000 earth tons after orbital launch from Mars base. That's approximately well over 6 million earth pounds considering the amount of extra chemical propellant it contained to one day be used to launch the probe homeward to planet Earth.

After all, it is and was Esthrep's main programming, to explore the Sirius system and if possible in a final quest for humankind, to return that gained information back to it's home world called planet Earth.

Esthrep now reversed and engaged it's engines toward their forward path and began using a portion of their chemical propellant to slow the craft for orbital attempt ahead.

Since the journey from Triderious. Esthrep had trained its solar receptors toward the inner bright sun to recharge it's electrical and nuclear defense system in case it was ever needed.

As small in size as the planet Crattius was. It rotated on its axis very rapidly once every eight hours twenty two minutes earth time.

The liquid water that was detected from a distance was scarce but certainly substantial enough for a civilization of Cratts to exist.

The sixth hour point of decelerating to orbit speed, Esthrep was suddenly surprised by another instantly appearing Cratt orbital defense satellite.

This time the crew elected to remain detectable and face the Cratt society full out.

The crew rightly figured this was to be the most important exploration yet and that their survival hopes now rested on the abilities of the entire crew with Esthrep as the lead encounter representation of humans best technology to this present star date.

This scout probe again grasped Esthrep by its forward nose ring and immediately proceeded towing Esthrep towards the Cratt planet.

At this point the entire crew had chosen to not resist the capture in order to save any weapons that they had disguised and hopefully never having to employ them.

Deep in Esthrep's programming there was a self destruct mode that hopefully would never have to used.

The towing Cratt craft orbited the planet at a three hundred kilometer altitude.

After a time span that the Cratts deliberately controlled, their view screens suddenly became active and displayed a fierce looking large Cratt creature. The crew found it extremely hard to describe the creature in human earth words.

The Cratt creature image screeched a horrific roar before the ships interpreter could translate it into English.

Stop it screeched, We the Cratt society have detected that you came from the direction of the Drog planet Triderious

The roaring words then threatened the destruction of Esthrep if full surrender was not immediately complied with.

After a short pause the crew surrendered their ships future into the hands of the Cratts whom soon they were to meet on a realistic personal experience each their own.

Directly under the Cratt's control, the crew were now energized again and stood directly below the knees of the Queen of Cratt's.

CHAPTER 29
BELLA THE CRATT QUEEN

Garbed in a Drog skin decorated robe, the female Cratt creature screeched a not yet translated sound towards the human projections.

She stood eleven feet tall in a single cathedral alien exotic chamber with two of the Queens meanest ugly looking male muscle guards standing silent and armed with weapons.

Real humans of Earth would have never been able to withstand the extreme gravity of Cratt. Being a human projection, the gravity didn't affect the human holographs because truly, their biological essence still existed with the Esthrep Main in orbit.

The Queen Cratt stood on her rear knobby legs that were jointed but budging with extreme muscle mass.

Her cloak the color of golden solar rays leading up to her head that revealed the prying snarling feline angry eyes that she had.

The two guard creatures were huge too but the Queen that they stood beside was almost a human head and a half taller than the Queens own two huge muscle guards.

The Queen was glamorously adorned in appropriate attire and now addressed the six human holographs loudly with a roar.

The message translated to sit and listen. Do not interrupt! The human holographs knew that sitting was not ever needed for their holographic nature but figured that accommodating the Queen's orders, was the best thing to do at this moment of first contact with the Cratts.

The humans expressed meekly that the loudness of the Queen's roars were unnecessary and pleadingly asked that they be spoken to in a lower tone for easier comprehension by earth human representatives from the planet Earth.

Her next roar was half the decibel tone but extremely forward in its orders to comply and explain their presence here.

The crew took turns in replying to the huge catlike Queen of Crattius. She then stated her designation as Queen Bella of Crattius.

She demanded loudly again, for an explanation of their visit to the Drog planet.

The first human spoke up.

Yes we explored the Drog world on our way inward here to Crattius but we take no sides in the war that has existed for eons between yours and their species.

The second crew member spoke.

That being said, we humans from earth have assimilated the facts of your war in our home solar system eons ago and wish to discuss these occurrences and all the facts it entails.

Queen Bella roared again loudly chastising the human entities on their feeble braisonistic attitude and total disconcert for their ships well being in orbit.

I as Queen Bella could have your ship crushed at the snap of my claws and unless you reveal your intentions I will make it happen.

The holographic six alone were not susceptible to physical force but knew if the Esthrep probe in orbit were destroyed that they as earth reprehensive would cease to exist.

One at a time they spilled their intensions of garnering some sort of peace treaty between the Drogs and Cratts, using the long ago destruction the Drogs and Cratts did to the human's solar system as a forgiveness peace treaty leaf.

Queen Bella roared in anger at the mention of a peace treaty with the Drogs. She was totally against any peaceful intentions towards the Drogs.   She also knew very well that the Drogs hated the Cratts and always would.

This has always been the case, stated the angry Queen Bella. We could never have peace between our two cultures she exclaimed laughing at the disgusting earthling's proposal.

She continued with anger in her roar.

You Earthlings know nothing of Cratt, Drog matters and should mind your own business for your own sake.

We Cratts have no intention of ever conversing with these vile vicious Drogs about living in peace.

We've always had war and always will she exclaimed. Any possibility of a truce will forever remain impossible she ended with a vicious snarled roaring purr.

Silent seconds passed before a member of the Esthrep crew replied.

Queen Bella, We're here representing the human race.

We do realize that we're not welcome in any sort of peace talks but, We've also conversed with the Drogs and they too are just as stubborn against your Crattius world.

If only there were some way that an emissary from both worlds could sit down and face each other without animosity and hate towards each other.

If only there was a way many Cratts and Drogs lives could be spared in future conflicts.

We Queen Bella, are only a hieroglyphic representation of the human race. We've now learned about the destruction that took place eons ago in our solar system between the Cratts and the Drogs.

Several planets in our solar system are forever changed by the wars of that day.

So you see Queen Bella, we six projections of humans, certainly do have a complaint against these forever wars between your society and the Drogs. We think that this should all end.

On Earth, Dogs and Cats live with human families inside their dwellings and many are trained not to fight with each other. In fact some animals have become good friends.

Queen Bella bellowed loudly at the end of their feeble quest for peace.

Do you humans think that you can come in here and barter a peace between lethal aliens and cause our nature to change overnight?

You pitiful frail beings must be out of your human duplicated minds.

I, or any other Cratt could never sit down in the same room that a Drog occupied. She growled another sign of disgust at the mere proposition of such a thing ever happening.

The Queen paced around her guarded silk like throne paused and then took a much softer attitude towards the humans.

It's true she stated. The war did cause a lot of damage to two planets in your solar system many eons ago. Even Earth itself was altered in those days because of both of our presence in your solar system. The Planet Venus itself was mostly destroyed by the use of now outlawed lethal chemicals of that time period.

Our laser and nuclear weapons at one time of the war, ignited the atmosphere of Venus and forever changed any possibility of it ever supporting life.

It also caused the planets magnetic field to almost disappear resulting in the planet flipping upside down and why it now rotates slowly westward.

The wars around Mars also changed that early developing world and caused the planet to lose it's water and most of it's developing atmosphere.

The Cratt Queen Bella spoke softer now with a more even conciliatory voice.

Mars was once a very welcoming environment world to us Cratts. Bella regressed back to her great grandmothers ancestors records about a monkey like creature that lived on Mars before their war began.

Some were large and some were small monkey creatures she pondered. There were also many rat like critters that burrowed the rich oxygen soil of that long ago Mars Planet.

Some of the surviving species were transported to Earth in it's thawing days after the great ice comet destruction of your then Earth.

Our ancestors Cratts also injected our DNA into a ferrule mole creature that emerged before the slow freezing of those cold Earth days.

Soon after those ancient days, The Cratt species returned back to our home Crattius Planet.

A temporary truce was enacted but it lasted only a short while.

Queen Bella regressed in memory further back when she was reading the first recorded history of her earliest ancestors writings.

There once was a time long long ago, when Drogs and Cratts lived peacefully and shared the same self awareness that all creatures should have towards each other.

There was a long ago era that Cratts respected the existence of Drogs.

In those days both societies respected each others territories and got along just fine.

The Queen then was a young Cratt when she first discovered the archives and pondered at that time of youth, that this was a delightful concept.

The realityy of a world that she knew at present time, would never agree to such a silly things as Drogs and Cratts possibly living peacefully in the same planet double star system.

She sniff chuckled under her breath a bit after the memory of the chronicles of history came back to her mind.

You know what she exclaimed to the human crew in a question.

Perhaps I the Queen am now intelligent enough to realize that war is a ridiculous concept. No matter what reasons are given.

The Queen snarled and then bellowed.

Tell your Drog friends that I Queen Bella, am willing to have a peaceful talks with Drogs of the planet Triderious.

Only if they agree to the peace conference also.

The Humans would be designated as arbiters before the summit is to begin she declared.

With that grand accomplishment, the humans were delighted at the outcome of the Cratts willingness to trust them in speaking for their worlds interest.

On the voyage here, nearly midway between the Cratt's planet and Triderious, An agreed to summit was scheduled to take place between The Cratts and the Drogs.

The message was relayed ahead to the Drogs and would arrive at Triderious in six and a half light hours time.

The six were returned to their chambers aboard Esthrep and now awaited a reply from the Drog planet Triderious.

They understood that Drogs were stubborn but explained with great detail the importance of this accord for the benefit of both Drogs, Cratts and Human matters of the no war attitudes.

In sixteen hours and eighteen minutes, they received a reply from the head council of Triderious, King Revoris.

It was short but to the direct point., The message read.

We accept this opportunity to sit down with talks between I Revoris and Queen Bella of Cratt.

In the hours that followed, an agreed upon time for the conference was decided to be held halfway between the two planets in 28 earth days time.

The conference would take place on board a Cratt ship due to the fact of the large size of the Cratts and Drogs.

Each represented party would be allowed only two guards each and the Esthrep probe's crew would serve as the arbitrator to the peace talks.

One rule, No weapons allowed.

All was set for the peace talks between worlds in the three star Sirius system.

There would soon possibly be a truce or maybe not.

Esthrep the probe may even get destroyed in the attempt to interfere with natures rage but one thing was in agreement among the Esthrep crew.

They had started this and they would try their best to make it happen.

Even if it caused more war, they had to try. To much was at stake. Their own solar system had been changed by the alien wars of eons ago.

After learning the facts, the humans felt like they had a say in this matter also. Some things deserve to be made right. That was their combined thinking.

Days passed quickly as now on the specified day, two large crafts and the Esthrep probe arrived at the designated co ordinance agreed to by all parties involved.

CHAPTER 30
THE ARMISTICE ACCORD

The Cratt claw grappled Esthrep and the crew were energized inside the Cratt ship above a gleaning clear table between two throne chairs opposite a twenty meter diameter table.

Esthrep's crew floated gracefully above the grand table inside the huge Cratt ship.

The crew projected it's images in the middle of two giant thrones facing each others directions.

The clanking of metal was heard as the Drog ship now docked to the huge Cratt ship for the first time in history.

Depressurized hisses occurred and the hatch between ships slid open.

Out steps the Head Drog Revoris. Revoris stood three meters tall compared to the taller Queen Bella.

Revoris steps into the ship growls a bit and says nothing as he stepped to his awaited throne chair.

Now Revoris sat directly across facing Queen Bella. Their prying eyes met with disdainful looks and for a moment the Esthrep Crew though they would fight.

The Earth crew spoke up to break the tensions before either had a chance to react.

We're all here to solve problems and save lives. The Humans spoke as one voice.

We want you to know that the remains of both of your dna that was left behind on earth has developed into friendly human pets as cats and dogs.

Yes they do live together in human homes mostly if they have grown up together in the same households as humans.

Truthfully, there has always been animosity between cats and dogs on earth but somehow, most have learned to accept each other and live in peace.

The probe's combined voice continued with a few more opening statements.

We humans of earth wish that these hostilities between your parties would end in hopes of making all of us safer in the long run.

We agree that old habits are hard to change but all of our species are intelligent in their own developed ways. What is needed for all is a lasting fair peace agreement. No one needs to die from war anymore.

Revoris spoke up next a bit too brash at first but The King settled into the grips that he had against the Cratt society.

He stated further that in their defense, the Cratts had recently destroyed some of their scout robots in the mid distance system where they were placed at this approximate meeting point.

This angered Queen Bella at the indignation of the Drogs complaint because both sides had destroyed each others mid distance scout ships on many occasions.

She bellowed these facts towards the face of the Drog King Revoris

That may be true Revoris replied as the Queen settled back into her huge throne chair.

Both of our worlds have lost many souls and much time and resources fighting each other with nothing good that could ever be expected from results like the wars of our past.

Queen Bella butted in.

Both of our ancestors did great damage to two planets of the human's solar system.

Cratts and Drogs must come together and offer reparations to the humans of Sol.

King Revoris stood up in agreement stating, You're right, this fighting for eons has brought every being nothing but misery and strife. We do owe the humans reparations of both our ancestors war disaster to their Sol system.

If both of our left behind DNA species have developed acceptance of each other in their earthly existence, surely all parties here must agree that acceptance is something that has to be honored by all parties.

Trust is only sacred when it is pure truth.

Last but not least, both planets should pass laws that must be obeyed by each other.

Cratts and Drogs must from this day forth accept each other as equals among beings of intelligence.

For the first time in eons an agreement had been reached and paws shook around a grand 20 meter table with the Esthrep crew floating gently above the parties at conference.

Talks went even further on exchange of goods between worlds that both Cratts and Drogs could soon begin cargo runs between both planets while greatly increasing both of their worlds prosperity.

The Cratt ship was extremely large due to the size of the Cratt beings. Even so, the cargo bay where the conference was held was just large enough for the six large beings and projected crew that were in attendance.

Also amended to the agreement was a commitment from both parties in the near future to visit the humans solar system again and try to help restore some of the damage to Venus and Mars that their ancestors caused eons ago with their past war with each other.

Several more constructive talks were held and it came the time for all three parties involved to sign the total agreement of peace.

Esthrep's crew floated 10 meters above the crystal round table and across each side sat Queen Bella and King Revoris the head council of Triderious.

The Drogs appeared slightly smaller next to the larger Cratts but all seemed equal at the ceremony agreement of the signing of the new treaty.

Each party scribbled their version of a signature and Esthrep generated the seal of total agreement.

Esthrep was transmitting the signature of the seven aboard Esthrep and the Sirius Sol Treaty was to begin in forty eight earth hours.

Both worlds would be notified immediately and all hostilities should cease between the Cratts and Drogs. The six sentient Humans aboard Esthrep had accomplished a grand task.

Esthrep's main computer recorded the event and cast the final vote of approval to seal the treaty forever and a day.

Word spread quickly to both worlds of the new treaty and orders to respect each other were enforced.

Very few final squeamishness occurred and Cratts, Drogs and Humans began a new commitment.

Since the Drogs planet had already been visited by Esthrep's crew, word quickly spread to the Cratt planet that Queen Bella was returning soon with the human ship Esthrep to visit their world.

Esthrep looked very small in comparison along side the huge Cratt vessel that now approached the marble Crattius planet.

Both ships decelerated to gain proper speed to enable orbit a thousand kilometers above the golden marble colored world called Crattius.

Interesting facts were learned about the Cratts in rout to this journey.

Yes the Cratts were extremely big and the average Cratt's height was about twelve feet tall in human comparison.

Queen Bella herself was more than a half meter taller than most of her race. Few guards had the height and sheer muscles that the Queen possessed.

Unlike Earth's population of billions, The total Cratt population here was a mere six hundred thousand.

That's the Crat population in Queen Bella's words.

That's all we need. We are strong. Those were her final words before the welcoming scheduled for twelve hours away was to begin.

The six after recharge, awakened on command by Esthrep the main computer

The crew prepared for their holograms to be transmitted to the place of welcome designated by the Cratts.

CHAPTER 31
A VISIT TO CRATTIUS

The huge domed room suddenly revealed a hundred or more Cratt beings and the human holograms stood the center ring of its entirety.

Queen Bella stood on a slightly recessed floor a little below the human figures. She began introducing to the other Cratt's the humans that now all Cratt eyes curiously watched the funny looking creatures that they now beheld.

The tallest human was only two meters tall and several of the others were only a meter and a half.

They adorned the funniest apparel according to the laughter of several Cratt's in attendance.

The Cratts had never seen such creatures that stood the center of the giant room.

Chatter soon died down and Queen Bella spoke her introduction.

These are computer representations of humans from planet Earth in the Sol system. I Queen Bella bid them a gracious welcome as head barters of the peace treaty just signed with the Drogs. These are the projections of the human entities that inhabit their vessel in orbit above called Esthrep.

The Esthrep probe with these six entities journeyed here from Sol which is well over eight and a half light years distance away. The journey took them over twenty earth years to arrive in this three star system.

Now thanks to their help, a new peace treaty has been signed with the Drogs of Triderious. We are no longer at war. Drogs will be respected in future arrivals and any who break that treaty rule shall answer directly to I Queen Bella

The Queen's message was broadcast live to all who dwelled on Planet Cratt. Queen Bella finished with allowing the humans to speak and receive questions from appointed audience members.

Another female Cratts voice echoed through the translator as it came out into perfect English across the ears of the crew.

She asked of the humans, rumors have it that you have a animal on earth that you call cats and also a animal named dogs and they have learned to live among humans in peace.

Why yes, a female voice from the holograph answered immediately.

On Earth, most humans are larger than cats and dogs and many human families keep them both as company in the same home.

Her name was Trittimee and she responded with curiousness once again.

What are pets? That is something our society has never encountered.

Pets number 6 explained, were animals that are kept inside the home of humans on earth and are much loved creatures.

They also do many life saving tasks. There are actually police dogs that work on earth.

Pets are loved and well fed by humans and many people enjoy the love that is returned to them by the pets that they own.

An upset male Cratt loudly interrupted the earthlings response. Own he exclaimed with disgust, That's absurd. You can't own any creature or animal. It's against nature.

I think that you misunderstand a male voice of the probe replied.

On planet earth, most of these animals are small compared to the size of humans. In fact most cats are only six to twelve inches tall and walk on four pawed legs. That's absurd the Cratt Rinus now interjected his concern.

If that's the case, just how big are these pet dogs on planet earth? Well, a member of the probe answered, Most dogs on earth are much bigger than cats but you must understand the truth here.

There are more than one species of Cats that roam the wild lands of planet earth. There's a lion species that can grow to as many of three times the size of humans on earth.

Other species called tigers are huge and are wild meat eaters. There are several species of cats on earth but only the small kind are kept in homes by humans and most are loving pet animals.

It's against the law on planet earth to intentionally hurt cats or dogs or many other animals. Also birdlife are protected on earth.

Bird life protected exclaimed Rinus the Cratt. Here on Cratt birds are a deliciously toasted treat. We actually live off of the many foul animals that fly here on Cratt.

It was amazing to watch Revoris the Drog stumble around clumsily in the heavy gravity environment that all the Cratts lived under even on their ships.

The hologram humans were not affected at all being that their presence here was just a projection of who they actually were aboard the Esthrep probe.

Queen Bella interrupted the commotion and ordered the room to get quiet. They all listened with attentive ears to her next words.

Enough with the questions of our human visitors she proclaimed.

Tomorrow we invite the humans to visit Cratt and get to see it's many unique wonders. Let it be made so.

The Queen Bid the Drogs and Humans a courteous goodbye, then swiftly departed swirling her robe past the smaller human projections and she then disappeared instantly behind a flowing lit curtain.

King Revoris and his two Drogs returned to their ships after exiting the Cratt conference. The six human projections retreated back to recharged aboard Esthrep in readiness for tomorrows visit to the Cratt society.

CHAPTER 32
WHAT'S IT LIKE ON CRATT?

Esthrep Main duly captained away at the attitude control as the six humans awaited awakening in a few hours.

Esthrep the computer was just beginning to catch up recording and storing away all the data that the probe had assimilated up until this point in time.

Esthrep's processors slowed their labor as the task reached completion and its attention became devoted strictly to the probes attitude control.

Orbiting about one hundred miles above the surface was causing extreme havoc on Esthrep's welded ceramic frame.

The high gravity of Crattius was causing the ship to stretch and compress while it was this close in on the Crattius orbit.

Esthrep ascertained that a three thousand kilometer or 1864 mile high orbit would be much safer on the delicate hardware that Esthrep bore.

The Crew could still be transmitted safely from that distance.

Esthrep made the orbit maneuver and the crew was awakening upon orbit insertion completion.

Introduction to Cratt land was an exciting experience for the Esthrep Crew.

Giant dwellings filled their view as they glided along wide passageways on Cratt. It was amazing to watch the way the Cratts maneuvered around in the heavy gravity of their world.

The Cratts had huge transport hover vehicles. Their hover craft moved silently and swiftly as they flew each in different directions above ten meter wide roadways that also enabled a rolling ball cylinder ground vehicle to transport at slower speeds.

Up ahead as the long line roadway ran, you could begin to distinguish a city far away in the distance.

The heavy gravity didn't affect the human holographs that now rode the transit system among giants towards a planned destination.

It was revealed that the Cratts only populated three cities on the entire planet.

Each city was situated near the equator and existed at equal distance around the globe of Crattius.

Many large Cratt homes occupied single lots all along the journey towards the first Cratt City.

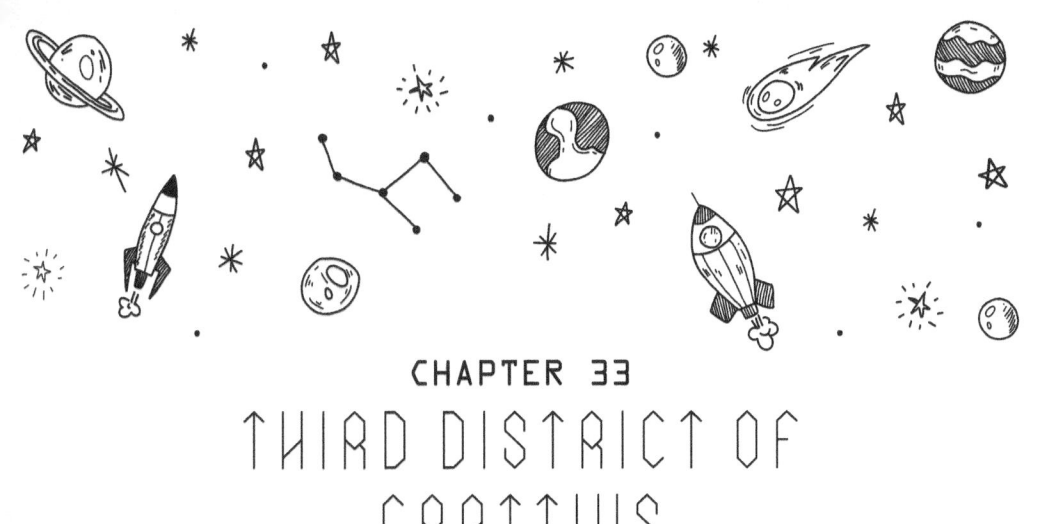

CHAPTER 33
THIRD DISTRICT OF CRATTIUS

The approaching city was entitled Third District by the inhabitants of Cratt. There was also second and first district cities that the crew would be allowed to visit later.

Third district was emasculate. There were grand castles with motes and street vehicles that resembled huge earth moving machines of earth.

Most were electric although a few did used a noisy smelly combustion engine as propulsion.

These vehicles were huge enough to carry four Cratt inhabitants if necessary.

Third Districts population consisted of approximately 200,000 Cratts. The floral pastures between castle dwellings were magnificently beautiful.

Many dwellings had crystallized green cat eye windows and four meter diameter circle shaped doors that magnified both ways a perception of size and detail.

Some dwellings were round 30 meter high and half ball dome shaped. Odd shaped transmitters were attached to the apex of many roof domes.

Dwellings for Cratts were huge.

Normal homes stood from thirty meters tall from their center apex.

Homes outside textures were as if made of a slightly fuzzy bubble pebbled surface.

Colors ranged the entire spectrum and under bright Sirius A's sunlight, there were many colors of everything.

A crimson yellow sky contained many scattered puffy purple white clouds. Sirius A appeared bright white yellow in the sky of Cratt and almost twice as big as the Earth's Sun from Earth would appear.

Sirius B was closer in but still only half as large as Earth's Sun.

It's rosy tint and heat to the Cratt Planet enabled life in this habitable zone of the Cratt Society. Even so, A's light was so bright, that B was almost obscured in the brilliance of Sirius A.

Atmospheric pressure here on Cratt consisted of 750 millibars or 75 percent earth pressure at sea level.

The difference is, that the atmosphere on Cratt consisted of 45 percent oxygen with 40 percent nitrogen, with the remaining 15 percent consisting of mostly carbon dioxide and a few other trace gases.

The Cratt Queen Bella had a grand celebration prepared to welcome the human hieroglyphs from Planet Earth.

It's not easy to explain but fires projected and appeared uniquely different on planet Crattius.

Queen Bella had prepared a three hour nighttime welcome to Cratt for the humans.

The grand enormous arena podium that the humans now stood upon, was surrounded on all sides by nearly three thousand large Cratts.

The Humans seemed so small as the six stood the center podium looking upward at the thousands of aliens.

Extreme quakes began shaking the arena as the Cratts promenaded their fire sticks that most had in their left paw hands.

The tips of their fire rods projected a cool violet light in all directions.

Blue green fire glowed twelve inches above their staffs and somehow no heat was being generated from their tips.

Their fire tip staffs when at rest were always the eye level height of the Cratt that was holding it.

The Cratts rumbled the stadium again by pounding their staffs in unison to a slow rhythm.

When they stopped pounding the floor, the flame settled gently then changed into a plasma blue cold short flame.

The Cratts staffs that they always carried, were as computers are to earthlings.

The Cratts processed everything through their worldwide internet through their staffs.

The Crew hardly ever saw a Cratt without one while they were on their world.

It was amazing to watch the large Cratt's move around but their muscular physique was always able to fight the strain of excess gravity.

The surface soil on Cratt was compacted to an extreme limit. It would be like digging in the soil with a pointed shovel and the shovel would be hitting solid concrete with every attempt at digging.

No Earth-like plants could ever grow here. What did grow on Cratt, were these 5 meter diameter, four meter tall round top trees that cracked the ground with thick purple roots.

If you got near one, you could smell oxygen being generated.

The Cratt trees did have a few short stubby limbs with mushroom looking leaves. The mushroom leaf tips tracked the B star in the planets short daytime cycle.

The trees always tracked the Cratt B star as it only took three hours and ten minutes to cross the crimson sky.

Cratt trees were spaced sporadically between the three district zones. Lands between trees showed a forest floor of venus fly trap looking plants that grew wild on Cratt.

Their visit to district two then on to district one was a stimulating experience also. The Cratt technology was incredible.

It seems the concentrated soil of the planet was also very easily used to make many things on planet Crattius. It made a type of metal that was as thin as aluminum foil on earth and easily used to build just about everything on Cratt.

The peculiar thing is, Cratts were not meat eaters.

They only had several food source requirements and that was the mushroom leaf pods that grew on the fat Cratt trees and the fly trap garden vegetables that grew wild between the forest trees.

Those were the tree mushroom leaf pods that gravity oozed oxygen out slowly. The leaves had such a high protein nectar content, that one leaf from a tree limb pod met the full requirement for one Cratt meal a day.

Cratts day cycles only lasted three hours and ten minutes. Most of the Cratts slept the three hour night period and were always awake at B's sunrise.

Cratt farmers harvested the fruit of the trees and forest floor vegetables and shipped them to all three districts.

It was amazing to watch a giant machine operated by a Cratt on the approach of a tree that it was harvesting. It moved slow while trimming and storing the floor vegetables as it approached a tree.

Then, a twenty meter tall machine arm reached out with two teethed belt like tongues and clipped the mushroom tree leaves off and then spliced the clipped area with a silky frazzled gold band aid patch in order to produce two new leaves in that spot in twenty seven Crattius days rotation.

There was another food grown their for consumption.

Farmed high up in mountain communities, there were Cratt families that made their livings harvesting this delicious to Cratts red bush plants that grew only in the mountains. Its petal flora smelled like a sweet cake bread.

The flora that sprouted in this two meter tall plant were very dense flowers of almost a dark purple color existing at the center.

Dozens of petals occupied each bush. Six rows of six in every farmers garden.

It was only allowed that each farmer and family could only have thirty six bushes of food flora.

The Cratts called the plant Fuma.

From this much demanded fuma fruit, there was made a liquid drink on Crattius called Fuma.

All of the Cratts consumed this liquid nectar daily. Fuma liquids was produced in factories and the fruit was cooked with a mixture of the heavy hydrogen waters of Cratt streams that made a remarkable drink that was all the liquid that Cratts ever needed to consume.

Each Cratt consumed about three quarts a day of the liquid along with other different food recipes made from Fuma.

Cratts entertainment consisted of barroom like quarters with Fuma drinks and female Cratt servers. .

Cratts all had tails that they manipulated with delicacy like human finger tips.

Cratt males could carry two quarts of Fuma drink in their paws and snap grab females with their tails in passing.

Many became Fuma filled in passion's lust in an instant of a Cratts Life. .

Clocks mechanisms on Cratt were tuned to the six hour twenty minute rotation rate of Cratt.

Cratt days and nights were split up into six equal sections each called a cistern. Each cistern was a hour and three minutes converted into earth time.

Esthrep probe had set it's chronographs to the Cratt planet on first arrival. The had now visited Cratt for 94 cisterns of Cratt's cycles.

A great deal of new knowledge was accumulated.

The Crew regenerated while uploaded data into Esthrep's computer bank storage.

The Cratt's furnished extra chemical fuel and materials for the Esthrep probe in orbit and helped the probe rebuild failing necessary parts for it's return voyage home.

There was a meeting set up at an outpost half way between Cratt and Triderious to show their appreciation to the human probe Esthrep and Crew.

Many Drogs and Cratts were there to witness their departure. Both races had also signed an extension treaty to begin reparations to Mars and Venus in the Human's solar system.

Soon they would return back to the Solar system to report to Earth about their discoveries about the Dog star system called Sirius.

Eight point six light years travel time to Sol at one half light speed, it would take the Esthrep. Twenty three point eight years travel time.

It would take the Esthrep Probe nearly a full earth year to reach one half light speed making the return trip home to be about twenty four and a half earth years time.

They had spent three hundred and eighty days in the Sirius systems and if the probe was successful in it's return to Earth, a total of forty four Earth years aboard the probe time would have passed since their launch from Mars base.

But, that was Esthrep's time aboard the probe. Due to Einstein's equation of time dilation at fast moving speeds, over six hundred years will have passed back on Planet Earth when they return home.

Back on Earth in the solar system, according to Esthrep time line, it should be 2187 when they returned home.

According to that time line Esthrep probe had been away for a little over forty seven and a half years.

But, Even at Esthrep's half light travel speed here, Esthrep had indeed turned itself into a time machine.

Planet Earth and Mars base had never forgotten about the long ago launch of the Esthrep probe to the Sirius system. Flesh and blood humans could only wait patiently to see if the probe ever returned.

Little did Planet Earth know that far away in the Sirius system of stars and planets, that Esthrep was soon being launched back towards home.

Back at the launch outpost between Triderious and Cratt, a grand send off was given to the Esthrep probe and crew as they sailed away from the Drogs and Cratts. The Cratts and Drogs had reengineered Esthrep's engines to allow the probe to travel again at one half light speed

CHAPTER 34
HEADED HOME TO SOL

Esthrep began gradually gaining speed so that in one years time the ship would have reached it's top cruising speed of 93,500 miles traveled every second that is just a fraction over half light speed.

Two days out from the outpost, Esthrep had only managed to obtain a speed of fifty miles per. second.

It's speed would increase daily until it reached its maximum cursing speed. Then the nuclear ion engines would engage and Esthrep in six months time would be propelled to approximately 46,500 miles per second or one quarter light speed.

The nuclear ion engines that used a specific fuel called dithariam was its new reengineered power source.

The Cratts and Drogs had reengineered Esthrep's nuclear ion engines in order to help them get home to Earth.

The fuel was made from the rich dense surface mineral of Cratt. The engines were redesigned by the Drogs in cooperation with Esthrep's input and the Cratts furnished the fuel supply.

To break out again past Colossus the ice giant, the Esthrep probe had to fire it'd nuclear engines in order to increase the probes speed to approximately ninety eight miles per second.

That trajectory and speed would allow them to fall in behind and use the ice giant's gravity to slingshot the probe behind Colossus and break through the outer shock wave that these three stars caused as they orbited the Milky Way in the same direction as Earth's Solar system did.

Suddenly, there was a massive jolt to the probe as Esthrep instantly morphed it's shape and blue flames pushed the crew's ceramic modules.

The crew encased now by soft foam, handled the sudden forward speed change increased. The G forced went from zero to four G's.

The forward view was filled with the electric cold world of Colossus. For nearly an hour the engines continued to fire its resistance towards the large white cold crackling Sirius C.

The ice sun continuously grew larger by the second. Esthrep's welds and bolts were feeling the strain as Sirius C was flinging the probe at a tremendous speed closely behind Colossus's forward orbital path.

The G forces were now increasing from four G's to about ten G's aboard Esthrep.

Using Colossus's gravity, the probe would gain the total 108 miles per. second speed required to break through the inner bowshock wave that exist way past the edge of this systems own version of an Oort cloud of comets and rocks far past Colossus C.

As the probe approached the final seconds of it's sling shot maneuver, Esthrep was now traveling 96 miles per second and vibrating fiercely at ever point.

The speed and gravity increased by the second as Colossus's heavy gravity tugged it's frightful grip on Esthrep's atoms.

The six orbs aboard had been placed inside protective foam and processed safely into recharge stasis mode.

Their crystal orbs could withstand the extreme high gravity but the only way the occupants could survive was that they must be incased inside thick foam while the probe was in the slingshot maneuver.

Six Crystal orbs went semi dark as Esthrep main again sat alone at the controls.

Silence filled the cabin as the roar of the engines suddenly ceased firing and the view screen was full with the Colossus giant below.

Esthrep monitored the gravity fall as the ship was catapulted with a fierce snap around the back side of Colossus C.

Again there was a sudden shock of excess gravity as the nuclear engines again fired their thrust.

Nineteen and a half G's the cushioned orbs rested pressed deep in foam material as the final twenty G high gravity mark was reached.

For twelve more minutes the rockets spat fire then abruptly shut down as the ship left Colossus traveling the escape velocity of 108 miles every second.

The creaks and groans of the probe subsided as gravity settled down to zero.

Now it was up to the Ion propulsion that would gradually increase their speed by the day.

Once more in eight days time, the nuclear ion engines would be required to give them final exit speed to completely leave the vicinity of the entire Sirius system.

That was a slight increase in thrust by the ion engine. The new fuel technology was reengineered by the Cratts and Drogs to help Esthrep get home.

Esthrep again revived the crew in order to discuss the upload that still had many years to completion before all six experiences could be assimilated and stored safely away in Esthrep's memory banks.

Twelve days out now the probe approached the outer Oort cloud of ice and gravel rocks that orbited the outer edge of this three star Sirius system.

Some ice chunks were as large as mountains and at the speed Esthrep was traveling, frozen ice blurs of near misses sailed by the craft at incredible speeds.

Pings could be heard through the hull as tiny space particles made it through the shields and collided with the probes outer surface.

Another electric magnetic shield was then deployed to repel and destroy more incoming particles.

Masterfully, with Esthrep's proficient radar, it was able to pass through the million mile diameter belt with little damage to the probe.

Esthrep had lost atmospheric pressure due to several punctures in it's pressurized hull.

Two remaining Esthrepobots were immediately launched to repair slight hull damage that was detected.

A total of six hours and eight robot repair sorties later, the Esthrepobots meticulous labor was complete and the probe was again building up required atmospheric pressure inside the ships main quarters.

The crew were ecstatic with the total knowledge accumulated on this voyage, It would take years to back up the downloaded data in each of their memory banks.

They'd have to recharge and record for long hours and days to accomplish this task of uploading their experiences.

So much to tell here. If only they could reach Earth and tell all there is to know about the Sirius A,B,C, system and their discovered inhabitants.

Approaching thirty three days out from the outpost the Esthrep was traveling at a speed of 108 miles per second.

The forward main probe was now detecting the outer edge of the bowshock wave.

The crew again retired to stasis. Esthrep's nuclear engines spat their fire propelling the probe faster by the second.

It was calculated that they needed to reach 110 miles per second in order to break through the bowshock wave and completely leave the outer edge of the Sirius system.

For three hours the engines fired their might rearward as Esthrep monitored the progress from his alone 5 meter diameter crystal pod.

Approaching the near end of the engines firing Esthrep was satisfied that the ship had gained the proper speed for bowshock penetration.

Esthrep silenced the engines and its speed was now 111, miles per second. The craft's shield energized again as it punched through the outer bow shock's high magnetic field and solar wind.

For nearly two long minutes the probe groaned and shook as if it had splashed through a hot cloud-ocean of hazardous fire that produced extreme heat to the nose hull of Esthrep.

As quickly as it had started, 90 seconds later, the friction relented and the probe now sailed in silence gradually gaining speed now from its ion engines.

Esthrep was free from Sirius influence and on the way home.

It would take nearly twenty four years or so but if all went well, They'd arrive at Mars base again.

Esthrep could not have possibly conceived what would challenge their homeward voyage next.

Possibly, it could have been better prepared for the surprise encounter that awaited ahead.

Three months out now from Sirius launch outpost. The ship had reached a speed of 20,000 miles per second and the ion engines glowed at their tips while gradually increasing the speed of the Esthrep probe in the silence of space.

CHAPTER 35
UNEXPECTED ENCOUNTER

Luckily the crew were in recharge mode when two days later a surge struck the forward nose of Esthrep's probe with no shields deployed.

The craft shook with vigorous vibrations as the probe changed direction against its will. It was now falling a tedious parabolic curvature vector.

Esthrep disabled the ion engines in hopes to reduce the stress of the strong pull force that was causing Esthrep's bolts, screws and welds to be under stress.

There then appeared impressions of a ships silhouette.

The approaching alien craft was the source that emanated its laser towards Esthrep causing a strong gravity grip that now had the Esthrep probe under the alien ships control.

Minutes passed as it pulled the probe up close to a huge round ship as large as a five mile diameter globe of pulsing blue hot energy.

Flashes of colored spectral lights now filled the cabin where Esthrep was confined in its 5 meter crystal ceramic orb.

The projected colored lights was a probe originating from the alien ship.

In the beginning, no contact was made other than the data probes but eventually Esthrep received a message that had to be translated.

It took the probe nearly a day to break the decipher code but eventually Esthrep finished the task.

Based on a math code of fourteen. Esthrep finally figured the right process to translate the message into English. The crew were awakened and informed of the message content and their present situation.

CHAPTER 36

MESSAGE CONTENT !

Disarm Weapons We will enter.

A smell of burning metal filled the cabin as the crew tried to assimilate their present situation.

A bright torch was burning around the hatch door as they all watched in harrowed concern.

With a swish the hatch door burst open on its hinges from the inside pressure.

Their stood an alien that was indescribable at first. The rest of the pressure blew the remaining smoke away, there stood a meter tall teardrop head Grey alien.

It's outer skin glowed from the protective invisible electronic suit it wore in the vacuum of space.

Small delicate knobby arms as limbs with seven finger digits on each tiny gray hand.

For its body size, it had a large head supported by a thin neck and the face revealed large black teardrop shaped eyes.

Four alien eyes darted into the interior as their suction feet allowed the two of them to roam the cabin in attempts to verify that no threat or physical bodies existed aboard.

Esthrep Main, again quickly protected the crew by cloaking their presence with the fail safe computer program installed.

One alien Grey now stood forward alone beside Esthrep Main while the other investigated the six orbs.

The alien near Esthrep was deeply eyeing the 5 meter globe that Esthrep's core existence inhabited.

Fourteen tiny alien fingers rubbed the crystal ball's surface in various attempts to analyze the gold liquid filled globe in detail.

Esthrep could detect the high brain activity that the alien was ingesting into its system.

Every probe made was a challenge for Esthrep to outmaneuver the aliens attempt to discover the reason for Esthrep's existence.

Esthrep had also loaded the Drog and Cratt chronicles away in a secret file never to be found by intruders.

Esthrep through reverse probes using the aliens own data screen was able to ascertain some information about the alien Grey that stood inquisitively just outside its orb.

Yes they were gray in color but their race called their selves the Grey's and they pronounced the word Grey as Greee.

One's name was translated to English as best possible to Quanta who piloted the vessel that had Esthrep captured.

The Grey's came from the far off Alpha Centauri system looking for rare minerals.

The Greys extreme technology allowed their race to travel at fifty times the speed of light.

That's fifty times 186,000 miles per. second.

That's equivalent to 9,300,000 miles per. second. ,

On this specific considered short trips, the Greys could actually arrive several instances before they even left their departure point. Truly remarkable time travel at its best.

Esthrep could detect that this race was a class one society and was extremely advanced. Esthrep's processors were maxed out at deep attempts to stay ahead of the probing Grey alien Quanta's attempt to find out the inner resources of Esthrep's intentions and secrets.

It seemed that after a while, Esthrep sensed an easing of the probes attempts as if the alien itself had grown frustrated at attempts to unlock the probes secrets.

Quanta turned as his head bobbled slightly and eyes blinked twice. It took one more look around then floated towards the hatch door that it had entered while grabbing the frame of the hatch to stop it's forward momentum.

As easily as the alien Grey had cut the door open and made entry, it now welded in seconds the damage it had made upon entry.

Esthrep watched as both Greys floated towards a hatch on their own vessel.

After several minutes the hatch was sealed and Esthrep was released and its coarse towards Earth was corrected and continued.

The Grey's hadn't stopped the ships forward speed They had only altered the probes course slightly. Quanta's ship had followed along a parallel coarse on the port side of Esthrep.

Now released from the magnetic grip of the Grey ship, Esthrep watched as the ship moved away slowly then there was a bright flash and the ship simply arrived somewhere else even before it had departed where the Esthrep probe was. Amazing technology.

Evidently the Grey's only discovered Esthrep by accident and was merely curious about such a far away satellite with very odd properties.

After departing from Esthrep Quanta's alien ship broadcast a curious decoded message back to the Esthrep.

The message was so sophisticated that it would take several years to decipher.

Brightly in a purge of powered light, The Grey ship was gone quicker than it had arrived.

Esthrep's data banks were deeply confused because it was if the Alien encounter never even happened even though Esthrep knew for sure that it had been experienced.

Was Esthrep dreaming or did his time chronograph only record three minutes and fourteen seconds since the Grey first appeared? That crazy occurrence seemed so impossible.

The computers own time chronograph had recorded a six hour twenty eight minute encounter with the alien named Quanta.

Somehow, six hours and twenty eight seconds of Earth time had been condensed into three minutes and fourteen seconds in alien time.

It seemed impossible but Esthrep knew that it had occurred just as his main computer had recorded it.

It was a conundrum that Esthrep and Crew would have to decipher this complicated message on it's long journey home to Earth.

Esthrep had ascertained that it had to do with the aliens ability to travel at fifty times the speed of light itself. But even that was an assumption.

Perhaps the warped space around them as they arrived at that speed also altered the time continuum of space itself.

In other words they the Grey's had precise use of worm hole technology that gave their race much deserved high status among many known beings.

The alien Quanta had left the probe a message cubicle chip that contained information about their home planet named Tradona from the Alpha Centauri system.

That's all that the probe had deciphered after a weeks travel since the encounter with Quanta the one meter tall Grey.

The message language was highly complex and slow to translate because of that sophisticated fact. These aliens had a very complex recording system of a highly complex base fourteen system technology.

Each word sometimes would take days to decipher because Esthrep could not configure the decimal difference between it's known base ten system and the aliens base fourteen system.

Actually, the message switched between several mathematical base systems making the decipher take much longer than expected.

The Grey's numeral system was figured precisely down to fourteen place holders and the translator decipher sequence had to be precise within three attempts or the number sequence would change again.

Once locked in, it could be repeated several times with the same letter conclusion.

The hard task was taking much of Esthrep's time but as the crew slept and recharged their experiences of recorded data, Esthrep had little else to do but tend the guidance of the ship and monitor the operation of the Ion propulsion engines that had now increased their speed to 82 thousand miles per second.

They were well on their way to achieving a homeward trajectory while the Ion engines glowed at their tips as they propelled the probe ever so gently faster by the second.

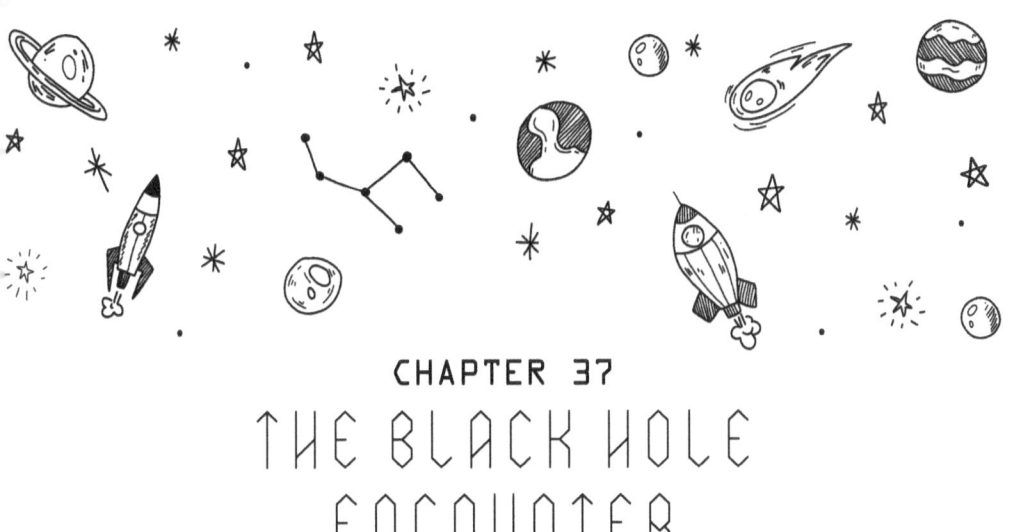

CHAPTER 37
THE BLACK HOLE ENCOUNTER

An enlightenment occurred that was the most amazing thing. From hence forth, all shall be referred to as the Probe or Esthrep. It speaks for all from now on.

The Crew was suddenly put into recharge sleep mode as Esthrep suddenly encountered an unknown power source from outside the probe. Opening up directly in front of Esthrep was a black hole swirling tunnel.

Esthrep's speed and course now vectored at high velocity towards a pinpoint golden light at the far end of a black rotating starlit tunnel.

Esthrep felt as if instead of falling, that a strong unknown force was pushing the probe at an accelerating speed towards a golden sunlit system at the very far end of the tunnel with blackness and starlight swirling all around.

Esthrep's time chronometer was reversing its past as if to say it was running backwards.

There was no way to time the sequence but to Esthrep as the Crew slept it seemed as if it was in a total reboot mode for days.

Exploding through the darkness of a rotating black tube, Esthrep burst through to a sparkling system of beautiful worlds orbiting a golden stars sun.

The blackness of the tube disappeared and the speed now had the probe slowed down and cursing at a slow rate of approximately fifty kilometers a second in this brilliant new system of planets.

Esthrep woke the crew as they stared ahead in astonishment.

CHAPTER 38

THE ROYGBIV SYSTEM

Ahead were seven equal sized heavenly bodies all orbiting equally spaced around a golden star.

It was indeed astonishing.

Each world approximately eight thousand kilometers in diameter and all colors of the spectrum were represented by each individual planet

The first planet inspected was red. The next orange, then yellow, green, blue, indigo, and violet.

The spectral globes were equally space around a golden star that was twice the size of Earth.

The brigade of spectral planets orbited the star in the same orbit equal spaced approximately three hundred million miles or 482 million kilometers from the golden star.

A rainbow of light touched each planet as the light bounded and lit up the immediate outward environment of the space it occupied.

The Esthrep probe sailed high over the north pole of this golden sun as the Probes guidance system pointed the ship towards the counter clockwise orbit of the remarkable seven worlds below their path.

All seven of these 8,000 kilometer diameter worlds had different atmospheres that reflected and displayed the remarkable golden sunlight that was shinning upon them.

Esthrep approached behind the orbit of the red world. It dispatched a robot probe to enter the atmosphere and act as a flying drone to examine the atmosphere and surface beneath the red clouds.

Smokey red dust was displayed as the drones visual projector fell trough the upper atmosphere and soon activated it's wings as it's speed fell to sailing speed.

Red clouds thinned as a misty red lit surface was revealed to the probes crew.

There were huge beast that roamed along steaming waters that were feeding on red vegetation trees along their path.

Different sized critters filled the red forest and the most beautiful birds ruled their surroundings.

Gravity here measured about sixty percent of earth's gravity and large beautiful plumed birds were perched atop many thick red tall trees.

There were green waters running through streams surrounding by thick 60 meter tall red bark trees.

The huge trees were displayed in the soft red color of the shaded sun shinning through the atmosphere and leaves above.

There were huge fat legged creatures that roamed in herds along flowing green stream river edges.

Tall grasshopper creatures gobbled at the tops of trees while huge feathered foul battled them for their defense of territory domain.

Atmospheric pressure was approximately two thirds earth pressure and as red as it was it contained mostly oxygen and nitrogen with a ten percent carbon dioxide content.

It was where the planet was in its orbit around the star that caused the atmosphere to be red.

Each planet changed it's colors from red to violet depending where it was in orbit around this golden star.

They each went through the ROYGBIV color spectrum as they the seven planets were in certain parts of their fifty earth year revolve around this golden Sun system.

It was if the golden star was projecting the spectrum in seven different directions.

CHAPTER 39

ROCKING SPECTRAL WORLDS

The star was named Golden A, by the crew and it's seven worlds all sequenced to alphabet musical terms ABCDEFG.

It was amazing to watch the seven worlds rotating on a sixteen hour period. When the first rotated eastward, it rotated once and reversed to westward. The next planet behind in orbit would reverse its rotation and begin rotating eastward. Then the third planet in sequence back to opposite rotation. Each forward planet controlled the reverse rotation of the other in orbit.

That's when the probe detected the real Jewel of worlds besides the seven rocking planets.

Esthrep had discovered that the eighth planet revolved around the golden star ninety degrees to the ecliptic of the seven color changing planets that orbit.

Planet Jewel it was named and it orbited the stars north to south pole direction. It's diameter 12 thousand kilometers or about earth size and it orbited the golden star in the habitual zone approximately one hundred and fifty million miles, or 241 million kilometers, in the direction of the Golden Sun's poles.

Planet Jewel would pass within fifty million miles always falling between the eastward rotating worlds of A to G.

Each Planet Jewel five year perigee, would coincide with the lead planet approaching a specific location. Then the gold star would cause the approaching lead planet to reverse and start a new direction for the rest of the sixteen hour rotating rocking planets to follow each planet in sequence to reverse rotation.

To explain further would be as follows.

If you have seven equal reverse rotating planets orbiting in the same orbit, planet A rotates eastward , Planet B, westward , C Eastward, D westward, E, eastward, F, westward G, eastward which is also rotating Eastward in front of A.

That's the exact point that G powers A to repel and reverse the process and become a westward rotating planet each time that Planet Jewel passed inside the seven planets orbit at a ninety degree angle.

Planet Jewel would pass within fifty million miles inside between A and G planets and cause the A planet to reverse its eastward direction to westward therefore continuously changing the direction of rotation to each planet in sequence of Jewel's five year orbit around the golden sun.

As Planet Jewel passed between A and G its equator was rotating ninety degrees away from the rotating direction of planets A through G.

The crew watched the forward prediction cycle of the yearly orbits of all eight worlds with extreme amazement. No human could have ever dreamed that a system like this existed anywhere in the universe.

It was if planet Jewel was the King of all worlds and the seven five thousand mile diameter worlds that orbited on a ninety degree different plane, were moons controlled by the Earth sized Jewel's existence.

CHAPTER 40

PLANET JEWEL

Esthrep changed it's direction and began vectoring towards the Planet named Jewel.

This Earth sized heavenly body sparkled like gold diamonds of the full spectrum. The probe fell inward to investigate further.

Esthrep had to fire it's nuclear engines to change it's direction in such a drastic ninety degree orbit.

Now silenced, the engines reverted to the Ion mode and gradually gained enough speed to approach planet Jewel.

Jewel sparkled as it rotated it's twenty eight hour rotation. Puffy white clouds and a green sea and brown land masses appeared beneath the clouds.

It was the green sea that seemed to control the sparkle from the golden stars light. One can only imagine the beauty of golden sunlight reflecting off the dark green seas.

As Esthrep approached within 5 million miles distance behind planet Jewel, it's detectors were now discerning a curious unique feature.

Planet Jewel had a ring. Not a debris ring but a highly sophisticated orbiting space ring that circled the entire planet at it's equator.

Suddenly Esthrep experience a serious power surge and it immediately put the crew in protective sleep mode.

Esthrep sat alone again at the guidance control and was following planet Jewel in a direction that was against its will.

A magnetic hold had taken over the Esthrep's control and the Ion engines had at the same time shut down its propulsion.

Within five thousand miles behind Jewel, the attraction ceased and Esthrep now orbited Jewel due to no actions or intensions of its own.

From behind Esthrep, a glowing disk craft approached and projected a beam that paralyzed the probe in space high above Planet Jewel.

The alien craft approached within a hundred meters of Esthrep and stopped short as if to sniff and probe Esthrep's content and intentions.

Esthrep alone again, sat and pondered this new possibility of meeting another alien race of extremely intelligent beings.

The probe could again feel deep scanning of its memory banks and the back up drives of the concealed crew members was still intact and not yet detected.

Esthrep projected its memory to appear to be a lost derelict satellite. It wasn't long before the intruder probe was no longer interested and it released the magnetic attraction it had for Esthrep and floated gently away in search of other threatening attempts from outside sources.

Esthrep now orbited 5000 kilometers above Planet Jewel. The crew was now awake from its protective sleep mode, Esthrep informed them of what had just recently occurred.

A few hours later, a consensus had been made that the crew wanted to venture further and explore planet Jewel.

It was their combined belief that they were here to explore and record facts no matter the situation at hand.

Esthrep and Crew ventured on. Silently sailing to within a 150 kilometers away from the equatorial space ring.

Esthrep could see now that the huge ring itself appeared constructed from sort of a golden metal.

The tubular ring was approximately fifty meters in diameter and circled the entire planet in the direction of its rotation as far as one could see.

Now detected were various sized ships that appeared to be loading and unloading cargo at different ports around the circular space ring.

Esthrep slowly approached near one of the ports and remained stable just outside a unloading ship.

Esthrep observed as cargo floated inside a ring port from the ship, but it detected no signs of alien contact as of yet.

Then began a rude awakening for Esthrep. Shooting out of a parcel port came a craft that headed straight for Esthrep at a extremely fast speed.

The 20 meter diameter tug ship stopped just short of the probe and enabled a mechanical arm to capture the probe and began towing the probe slowly back towards the port it came from.

In the clasp of the smaller machine and being towed inside, Esthrep now had a good view inside of the rotating ring around Jewel.

There were farms of crops growing all around the inside diameter in all tubular directions.

Far ahead at another distant ports you could see bright lights as if there existed a more dense population.

The crew came forth with their hidden identities and offer their respect to their captors as the probes door was opened to meet the inhabitants for the first time.

CHAPTER 41
JEWEL'S INHABITANTS

Outside Esthrep's door, their stood three heavenly entities that is extremely hard to explain humanly.

Before the crew stood several two meter tall beings and a one meter tall creature and all three had birdlike angelic features.

Their unique faces had no ears. They did have tiny noses.

They glowed with the star's gold light all about their bodies. Each floated without their perches hardly ever touching any surface. They moved around quickly like human sized hummingbirds.

Three beautiful angelic glowing creatures floated inside the Esthrep probe.

Two were almost two meters tall and one was barely a meter tall.

As they moved they produced soft tingling noises. They floated around the hieroglyphic crew that now introduced themselves as apostils from Earth.

After a few minutes of time the capturers had figured out the human language and a translation of the meeting was now being offered to the crew.

It began.

We are Jewelians from Planet Jewel. I am Diatina this other is designated as Tricera and the little one is Tai.

I Diatina have been appointed by our society to question you about your intentions in our planetary system around our Golden Star.

We detected your ship and technology when you first entered our system and have decided that you human replicas from Earth offer us no threat.

Its translated voices still had a tingle to it although it was completely understandable.

The Esthrep Crew replied in unison speech.

We are merely replicas of human beings from Earth. Our Technology allowed us to take a step into space exploration that ordinary living humans are not able to withstand.

We six in our globes were considered the best minds of our civilization. Only inside our Orbs are we really secure from harm and Esthrep the probes computer is our guidance and protector.

We are only here as explorers to learn what there is to be learned and if possible to someday return to our home planet and share all that has been assimilated.

The Crew asked permission from the Diatina to leave their orbs and show the Jewelians the real forms of human beings from Earth as holographs.

A tingling quick response was granted and the energizer beam now placed the six hieroglyphs from Earth directly in front of Diatina and Tricera and the little Tai that tingled at the sight it was now seeing.

Imagine seeing an alien for the first time. This was the delight of all especially Tai. We were the Aliens.

The Jewelians couldn't understand the two sexes of the human race. Their society consisted of only one sex. They reproduced by having partners but their eggs only bore one being inside its shell and any being was capable of reproducing.

They did have sex organs but they were all the same but their society did square off to have two partners to raise their young.

Maybe in Earth terms that would be considered Gay but this society had no concept of that sexuality. To them it was the only ever known Jewelian way.

Their planet below orbited the gold star once every five earth years. They measured their time in Quadals

A single Quadal was equivalent to approximately two hours earth time and 14 Quadals were the twenty eight hour daily rotation of planet Jewel.

Their year consisted of 25,550 Quadals and fourteen Quadals was equal to one Quada or what Earthlings would describe as one planet rotations time. A Quarter Quadal was equal to approximately thirty minutes in Earth time measure.

Each daytime period under the golden light star, was seven Quadals and also seven Quadals in its nighttime phase.

High above Jewel an outer ring existed 2,000 kilometers or 1,300 miles above the equator.

The partially completed lower ring which orbited about 1,600 kilometers or 1000 miles above Jewel, was joined from above with floating down tubes tow lines.

The floating long tube system continuously rotated in a belt like fashion from the upper ring's inside diameter that was controlling the speed of the completed section's construction of the lower ring.

Indeed this was a fascinating world with super intelligent beings.

It soon came to pass that many questions were asked and answered by both Jewelians and Humans.

The Humans hieroglyphs were cordially invited to visit the planet below and experience their society and learn more about the history and ways of life of the Jewelians.

The walls of the outer ring were semi opaque and the golden sun was visible to the crew as they decided to transport to the inner ring by the same method that the Jewelian inhabitants did.

The outer ring was indeed a complex cargo transfer station. Thousands of vessels all around the ring were loaded with material from an old rogue moon that was used to build the ring system.

The inner ring was still in its construction phase and a 50 meter diameter frame was being laid out ahead of the 30 percent construction that was already completed. The extended construction continued kilometers ahead revealing the circle frame with no skin attached to it as of yet.

A thousand or more Robotic Trods slowly moved around the outer edge of the fifty meter diameter ring tunnel. Like a moth building a cocoon. each trod slowly excreted a plastered smooth skin all around the ring frame as their entire progress measured about one half a kilometer per Quada.

Every Robot Trod cocoon builder was continuously being fed moon matter from hundreds of space tugs that ferried continuous sojourns from the moon to the outer ring port.

It had taken thousands of Jewel years for this society of Jewelians to have accomplished so much progress towards building a peaceful space faring society. To accomplish such a marvelous ring system built from the materials from a once rogue now tamed moon was remarkable.

The rogue Moon once was inching closer to Jewel before the tremendous removal of matter had decreased the moons gravity and now the moon was in a stable orbit behind Jewel.

Their society had calculated that it would take two thousand orbits around the gold star before the inner ring project was completed. That's about ten thousand earth years time.

The larger the inner ring became, the more moon material it required and it was estimated that the now fifty mile diameter rogue moon only contained enough matter to complete the inner ring to about eighty five percent completion.

That construction matter issue hadn't been solved yet by the Jewelians but their whole society prodded ahead with faith that a solution would be resolved in the future days here above Planet Jewel.

Thousands of train-like craft tugs and Jewelbots moved swiftly and methodically. The Jewelians worked vigorously towards one goal of shipping and receiving the processing of rogue moon matter. The Jewelians named the moon Rogue. They pronounced it as Ro-gue in English.

The crew were soon directed towards a down draft tunnel that would allow them access to the lower ring system that was partially built.

Floating ahead moved three angelic bird-like beings that leaped into a down draft air stream and quickly disappeared from view.

The Crew stepped upon the platform and leaped forward and watched the attendant above disappear down falling straight away.

It was as if they floated on a cloud but you could still sense the downward fall of static current rushing by as they were falling.

Earth holograms weren't susceptible to the effects of gravity but their sensors detected that a slight force of gravity now registered.

Two percent earth gravity quickly grew to six percent earth gravity before a soft slowing air cushion current occurred and a swishing air blast caused the system to stop abruptly but softly.

A door opened that slid them automatically out onto a solar lit floor inside the one third completed structure's lower ring of Planet Jewel.

Thousands of Jewelians labored under slight gravity to process moon matter and turn it into different compounds necessary to sustain life and make many different things on Jewel.

There was a thirty percent oxygen air content and 600 millibars pressure inside the lower one third completed ring.

Sounds of enormous industrial machinery could be heard all around the inner rings completed section.

The Jewelians were only slightly hindered by the light gravity and thousands of Jewelians could be observed hard at labor around machinery.

Guarded head attendants were called Jewelian Marshals at each station.

There were thousands of stations around all sides of the tubular ring as far as the human eye could see. The inner ring's completed section stretched a third of the way around Jewel and the sparkle of Planet Jewel below was a beautiful vision beyond spoken words.

Enormous amounts of twirtle sounding language occurred in unison as the inhabitants communicated on a grand scale with one another while performing their individual task of running their processing machines.

Out of the rogue moon matter the machines made a malleable space material paste that was used to construct the outer skin that was also a solar energy collector tuned efficiently to the gold stars power.

Obviously the entire process was very slow but the Jewelians labored on determined at their worthy task.

The entirety of all the machines only processed one kilometer of outer skin covering per Quada That Quada being equaled to 28 hours earth time.

At the present construction rate, it was calculated that it would take quite a long time to finish the inner ring construction project.

To be more precise, It will take nearly two thousand Jewel years or it will take approximately ten thousand earth years time to complete the inner ring.

The Jewelians had decided that when the Rogue Moon's matter would some Quada be depleted, construction of the inner ring would be mined from asteroids in order to finish the 15 percent remaining section's construction of the lower ring.

One more peculiar thing about the inner ring's center gravity point.

As the completed section rotated faster eastward below the slower rotating outer ring, the inner ring also rolled inward left and cork screw inward continuously changing the sixteen percent gravities center point as it turned.

Much vegetation and many grand gardens grew all around the inner ring. The rich smell of oxygen was indeed refreshing that was being produced from spiral forest of food gardens. As the completed section spiraled inward, it created a 16 percent gravity effect along the tubular walls.

Several Quadals had passed as the crew finished surveying the workings of the inner ring system and they decided that now was the time to investigate the Earth sized beautiful Planet Jewel below.

As the inner and outer rings were attached together with floating tube spokes, the journey to the planet below had no physical tube connections.

CHAPTER 42
DOWN PODS TO JEWEL

Each surface bound being was ejected from the lower ring inside a protective parachute contained electrical pod that gently transported them safely afoot upon Planet Jewel.

To transport to the surface below you would enter a clear all around egg capsule and were ejected downward to arrive in one quarter Quadals time or about thirty earth minutes.

The inner ring above grew smaller as they together descended through the upper atmosphere of Jewel. Stars in a gold lit sky became dimmer as their air egg sank closer to an awaiting port on the ground.

Eighty seven percent earth gravity was now recorded by the crew as their transport eggs gently placed them on a pad inside a busy immaculate crystal gold city.

The Golden Sun illuminated tall crystal reflecting tubular buildings that reached to the sky. The golden reflective streets that Jewelians traversed without vehicles were extremely crowded with inhabitants that moved swiftly and methodically along in their various destinations. They moved like hummingbirds only faster.

They lived in harmony. No wars had been fought and no political system was being used or wanted. They all accepted each other as individuals none more important than the other. The upper and lower cylinder rings grew many exotic fruits and vegetables that they ingested.

They had singular and multiple dwellings that they shared peacefully and willingly. The one meter tall young, played in protective gardens while the adults attended their duties.

The Jewelians gained their energy from the golden sunlight that lit the dayside of their existence.

Of the seven Quadals at night, four of those Quadals were spent in a sleep mode and the other three Quadals were used as entertainment time.

As far as the Earthlings could assimilate, this society had a perfect existence.

They had never had wars or didn't even understand the terms of hate that would allow destruction of property and lives. They had always gotten along in long past recorded times.

CHAPTER 43
THE ROGUE MOON CHRONICLES

The Jewel memory chronicles dated way back for several eons of time until the long ago recording of the rogue moon that entered their system and caused much havoc upon a long ago Planet Jewel.

The rogue moon once entered close behind planet Jewel and was captured by the planets gravity.

Many years of technology achievement had allowed the Jewelians of long ago the ability to create a space faring society that was able to begin harvesting the once two thousand kilometer diameter rogue moon. The rogue moon wasn't in orbit around Jewel. The moon after being captured by Jewel, was in a tag along path that at a long ago time was inching closer by the Quada.

The removal of moon matter to build the ring system had decreased the moons gravity resulting into a now stable distance behind Jewel.

Long ago tales of floods, mud slides and volcanoes and explosions were recorded in the beginning chronicles of Jewel's history.

Only a half of a million or so Jewelians survived the long ago rogue attack of the moon that was accidentally captured.

When first captured many eons ago, the moon passed to within a thousand kilometers in front of planet Jewel and caused extreme destruction.

Jewel's gravity captured the rogue moon and it eventually wound up in a tag along chase behind Planet Jewel.

It killed many of the Jewelians in the ancient days of the catastrophic encounter. The few thousand that survived fought long and hard to overcome the encounter of the past days of the rouge moon disaster.

In the early days after the first moon encounter, the remaining Jewelians developed their undersurface facilities and factories to begin the worthy goal of harvesting the rogue moons resources.

From the point of time of the Rogue Moon arrival, 1,860,000 earth years had passed since Planet Jewel first encountered the rogue moon.

From their early days until now, the survivors have been able to mine the rogue moons surface and process it's materials into a super nanotec plastered steel that was malleable under pressure and became light weight thin metal when it hardened in space.

In the immediate centuries thereafter, they that survival the struggle, began the building of the super light weight tube rings to be launched into orbit by harvesting the rogue moons resources and materials.

Once the first sections were completed, they were turned into processing modules in order to begin receiving moon matter directly from orbit.

Those long ago Quada now passed. The Jewelian society of angelic birdlike beings have created a marvelous double ring planet ring world.

The crew split up and began exploring the circle streets in the middle of each square block .

Each individually explored the Jewel society and all of it's glorious settings among this beautiful serene alien landscapes.

Atmosphere pressure here on Jewel was equal to two thirds earth pressure at sea level.

The twenty three percent oxygen content with 70% percent nitrogen left only a small percent of carbon dioxide, argon and other slight trace gases. It was very similar to Earth air . It's such a shame that real flesh humans weren't here to breath it.

Sounds echoed differently than if you were to hear the sounds under earth pressure. The combined twirtle language that all of the Julian's spoke was quite a pleasant sound as recorded in the exploration chronicles. .

The language sounded sort of like birds softly chirping with human words almost discernable.

It was a soft sound that seemed to be in harmony with the golden light of the star.

Nighttime vision of the skyline was breathtaking.

Soft lit see through column buildings emerged from the shadow of the planet. The golden star lit the inner ring and outer ring in reflected light.

The seven colored worlds that orbited the gold star at ninety degrees angle to Planet Jewel shinned their glorious brilliant spectral rainbow colors down upon the sixty degree Fahrenheit nighttime sky of planet Jewel.

It was once learned from one of the Jewelian citizens encounter, that the normal life span of a Julian was once in the long ago past only fifty Jewel orbits of the gold star.

While harvesting the different compounds of the rogue moons soil, A renowned physicist from the past had discovered an exotic compound that worked as a miracle medicine on their race. It had doubled life expectancy on Jewel to one hundred orbits of the gold light star. That's from two hundred fifty to five hundred earth years time.

Most same sex couples on Jewel bore two young children. One from each individual that habitated together. Habitation was also their word for sex.

They each could produce only one egg at a time and yes there were a slight percentage of couples that had as many as four siblings but the largest percentage per capita of the population had only two siblings per couple.

Some distance away from the skyward reaching buildings were forested water flowing gardens of emasculate beauty.

The gurgle of the flowing waters that surrounded solar collecting plants, pulsed under the golden rays of sunlight from above.

There were exotic green plants here but they continuously changed colors of the spectrum.

Wild flowers with odd shaped petals were strewn among the forest and water land scenery as far away from the city as one could view.

Thousands of Jewelian trees filled the forest floor.

The trees here were short and most only grew about four meters tall and none seen was any taller than the other.

It seemed these trees and plant life were the main source of the consumption of carbon dioxide and furnisher of oxygen in this alien but earth-like atmosphere.

The twelve feet tall thick alien trees were excreting high oxygen gas from spore looking leaves at the ends of short branches.

The ends of the branches appeared as if were gills on a fish.

Each tree had fifty or so gills at its tops and many more on its branches.

These tree-gills would change to blue as they exhaled their oxygen into the atmosphere wherever they grew.

Narrow streams of flowing green waters displayed different characteristics than flowing waters would on earth. Imagine that on earth a gallon of water weighs over seven pounds.

Water on Jewel was uniquely different. It had a higher H_2O content than earth water.

For one thing, atmosphere pressure here was a little over two thirds earth pressure at 750 millibars.

The same gallon volume of water on Planet Jewelian weighed about 10 earth pounds in the lighter gravity.

Water still sought the downhill of gravity but the flow was more jelly-like and slowed in its path.

There were many fifty meter or so wide pools of exotic swampy floral growth.

The sounds of flowing waters around them was extremely soothing in the soft winds of Planet Jewel.

There were also observed many forms of animal creatures that existed among the forest of the alien gill trees.

Several gorilla looking creature were seen eating gill leaves off the tree branches.

There were smaller creatures hover flying among the forest growth.

Many Jewelian inhabitants in the skies sailed the clouds with hummingbird like wings and precision due to the thinner atmosphere on Jewel.

The Jewelians were able to fly without need of mechanical devices. It was their way of life.

This Jewelian society had no perception of a government or any sort of a police state.

There was no hate or discrimination and the only war they had ever fought was the ongoing war with what remains of the rogue moon.

Here in the universe, was a peaceful society that had fought long and hard and won a frantic battle in order to survive.

They had taken the long ago tragic event of the rogue moon attack and turned it into a marvelous ring world planet called Jewel.

Day or night on planet Jewel, the ground existence and sky view was always exhilarating to the human senses. At certain times even in daylight, four of the seven ninety degree orbiting colored moons could be seen in the sky way past the outer ring systems edge.

The nighttime sky view was even more enhanced and spectacular. Many times here, human words seem incapable of describing the fullness of the contents of the Jewelian total environment.

At the center of every circle block, there existed a flowing water fountain.

Ten meters or so above the slow flowing jelly water fountain, there was a darker golden green entrance that Julian's had to either climb steps or fly in order to reach a dark golden flowing doorway.

The Jewelians would step through and be instantly transported anywhere on the planet or inside any part of the ring system above.

Humans couldn't comprehend this extreme transport technology but was fascinated by it's complexity and the fantastic technology of the Jewelians.

Half way into their visit to Jewel, the six of earth had to return to the Esthrep probe to recharge and fast record their experiences.

It was now informed to Esthrep by the Jewelians, that they now knew how to create a slight wormhole effect that would help launch the Esthrep probe back towards the same direction that had brought them here from Earth.

There was a stipulation that it had to occur at a certain time and that time would be here in three earth weeks time.

Esthrep's Main probe had been reconditioned and repaired by the Jewelian beings and the crew now slept charged for seven earth day periods.

They all awoke two weeks away from departure time and each wanted one more visit to the planet Jewel before they had to leave the beautiful planetary system.

There were exchanges of friendships and promises made to always remember their meetings here among the many stars of the universe.

Even though the earth humans had no physical bodies, their holograph representation gained high respect from all the Jewelians anywhere that the humans traveled on Planet Jewel.

One Jewelian school class wanted to know what Planet Earth was like.

They were then able to view a projected version of Earth and all the planets in the humans solar system.

The class was amazed that all the planets except Pluto orbited the orbited our star on the same equatorial plane. The also were Amazed by Uranus that tilted 90 degrees to the ecliptic.

In Jewelians young minds, they had always viewed the seven moons at a ninety degree orbital angle. The idea of planet earth having a yellow sun seemed so abnormal to them. The had difficulty imagining anything but their own golden sunlight.

The skies above Jewelian heads had always glowed with the soft gold rays of their golden light star.

They just couldn't comprehend the idea of planet Earth having fluffy white clouds and deep blue skies. or the fact that Earth was covered in two thirds salty blue sea water. All of their water was fresh water. Astronomy deeply fascinated the Jewelian young minds and they already had a lot of knowledge about the subject.

Planetarium sky existed past the almost clear connecting soft gold rotating spoke ring tubes that reached between rings in the heavens.

The crew had learned much about this futuristic society and there was much more to know but necessity prevailed.

Twenty earth hours from now, they would be launched back through the worm hole that Jewel scientist had created for the Earthlings launch towards home.

It's was imperative that in order to get the right worm hole the procedure had to occur at a specific time with not a second to spare.

The next Jewel morning, there was a grand ceremony from the Jewelian people to thank the earthlings and wish them well on their journey.

Many thanks were expressed by the humans and the knowledge gained here will fascinate the citizens of earth for decades. That is, if their journey home was successful.

Only a successful launch through the worm hole and precious time would answer that conundrum.

All goodbyes and well wishes attended to from both races, the crew each now reentered their one meter diameter crystal amino acid globes and went into a six hour recharge mode before the wormhole launch.

Esthrep Main sat patiently at the controls ready to command the launch attempt.

Esthrep had decided that it would be too dangerous for the crew to be awake as they were being transported through the worm hole and it let them stay in recharge mode past the launch time.

The Jewelians had placed the probe in the outer ring port and a focused warp beam that caused the space in front of the probe to extremely expand and connect to the same worm hole that the probe entered on.

There was no warning and instantly it was if the probe was falling at extreme speeds.

Then the probe was winding in a long clockwise swirl climbing then falling again.

For five earth measures of minutes Esthrep observed the walls of the probe to become distorted in and out of phase.

Clockwise it continued falling then climbing and spinning as they sailed. There eventually appeared a far away light glimmer at the far end of the spinning dark starlit funnel that the probe traveled through.

Esthrep fell even faster as the far light got much brighter and then there was a sudden burst through out of the end of the worm hole that sailed the probe into the blackness of starry space.

Esthrep was amazing that they were now back on course and they had gained a considerable amount of speed from the ejection of the worm holes power.

The Probe now traveling at eighty six thousand miles per second speed.

The worm hole shortcut ejection speed had increased the probes speed to a limit that no time was ever lost in their journey home.

The wormhole launch of the Jewelians society had actually cut their return home journey time to be approximately ten percent faster.

Seventeen years from planet Earth now the Ion engines had propelled the probe to eighty seven thousand miles per. second.

The probes estimated time of arrival back to Mars base was now down to approximately seventeen years at this present climbing rate of speed.

Top speed of ninety three thousand, and five hundred miles per second was estimated to be reached in about seven Earth months time. Now, in the seventh months later, Esthrep's Ion engines had succeeded in accomplishing the goal of a little over half light speed. The Ion engines were now shut down as the Probe's momentum sailed silently through the cold vacuum of deep space.

All was well aboard the Esthrep probe for seven years travel towards home until an occurrence at the nine year mark abruptly happened to the Esthrep probe.

There was a sudden shockwave jolt that struck the probe on its port side and caused all the computers aboard to shut down and reboot simultaneously.

Esthrep immediately put the crew in protective stasis until it could be ascertained as to what had just happened.

Again alone at the head, Esthrep Main had two wait for all of his systems to reboot before it could understand the circumstance that the probe now endured.

Time was of the essence but Esthrep Main's charge also had become nearly depleted and it's sleep mode had become a necessity to the probes survival.

For six months the entire probe slept. Far from the powers of their home sun, the probe had to rely on back up fuel cells to stay alive. Esthrep needed to reenergize and record their logs of a collision occurrence.

When Esthrep Main awoke from it's long needed recharge mode it became better aware of its present situation.

The probe was now inside a huge blimp type cloud chamber that was moving very fast also. It was a floating space cloud of dust that was super magnetically charged to a negative force.

Esthrep's Main computers were in continuous reboot mode due to the repulsive magnetic charge.

Esthrep used power to energized a magnetic field guard to the crew and the chronicle files of the past voyages in order to protect them from harmful radiation inside the cloud.

As the crew slept, Esthrep attempted to ascertain the total serious situation and figure out how to solve it.

Finally able to magnetically shield enough computers to activate sensors and guidance, Esthrep was able to estimate that they were moving along inside a huge space dust cloud and to it's edge was a distance of about a thousand kilometers away.

The Ion engines inside the cloud were non functional but Esthrep was able to engage one of the tree nuclear ion engines and navigate towards the clouds edge.

Tiny negative charged sparks bounced from Esthrep's forward tip as the one nuclear engine fired it's hot burst of flame rearward.

Bursting through the clouds edge Esthrep again reset its course and ascertained that the encounter with the cloud had added six months time to their journey home.

Now within a little over six years from home, the probe had completely recovered from the dust cloud encounter.

Members of the crew were still busy on scheduled recharge basis to continue uploading their personal memory banks into a back up archive file.

It would take four more years travel time for the crew to complete that long continuous task.

Thanks to the Jewelian revamp of Esthrep, The probe had traveled for years at ninety three thousand, five hundred miles traveled every second. That was just over half the speed of light.

The Probe would continue to coast homeward at this speed until it was approximately two years away from home.

At that point, the three nuclear engines would be required to begin the slowing of the Esthrep probe to a speed that would allow it to properly enter the solar systems bowshock wave and Oort cloud beyond.

Time smoothly passed more years until the probe reached two years away from the solar systems bowshock wave.

Still years from Mars base, extreme preparations were being made to slow the probe down in one years time away from bowshock encounter.

Traveling at one half light speed, the deceleration nuclear burn would have to occur for thirty continuous earth days in order to decrease their speed to ninety miles per second in order for the Ion engines to take over and make the probe able to slow down more in able to enter the solar systems outer magnetic bow shockwave safely.

CHAPTER 44
HOME'S BOWSHOCK ENCOUNTER

Eventually engine firing time arrived. All the crystal orbs including Esthrep, were cushioned into gravity foam in order to help absorb the shock of increased gravity during the thirty day firing of the Ion nuclear engines.

Esthrep's bowshock arrival time would be 8 months once the probe had been slowed enough to encounter bowshock. Esthrep's uranium nuclear core would be nearly depleted after the finale thirty day engine firing.

Rumbles echoed through the Probe as Esthrep now pointed its rear towards home and the three thunderous engines came to life one at a time.

For thirty days gravity was felt aboard the probe as it continuously slowed from half light speed.

Esthrep Main monitored as the crafts speed slowly counted down towards it's thirty day goal of ninety miles per second or 144 kilometers.

After seven hundred and twenty hours of nuclear engine firing, the gravity eventually reached five G's and began slowly climbing to the estimated six G level at engine cutoff.

From the point the engines shut down, the probe will be two earth year away from Mars base. Traveling at a speed of ninety miles per second, it would be up to the Ion engines to achieve their slow down speed of fifty five miles per second in order to safely break through the solar systems bow shockwave at the edge of their home solar system.

The past few years was an exciting time for all aboard the Esthrep probe.

Since the probe was launched, and due to the time shift of Einstein's theory of fast traveling objects, 637 Earth years had passed of Planet Earth's time. Esthrep had actually traveled to the future.

Their finale destination would be to arrive at Mars base stationed twenty thousand miles or 33 thousand kilometers in orbit around Mars.

Eight months passed by quietly as the Ion engines had succeeded in bringing the probes speed down to 58 miles per second. The Ion engines continued their slow reverse battle with the probes forward speed.

Working ever so gently against time and speed the energized Ion tips gave reverse propulsion in steady but slight power as the probe came nearer to the edge of their home solar system.

Their forward speed had been decreased to 57 miles per second when all the Ion engines suddenly shut down and lost all their power of reverse thrust.

Esthrep frantically sought a solution to the malfunction but it appeared that the main circuits had all burnt out on the Ion drives. Repair at this point was simply out of the question for the two remaining repair robots aboard ship.

At 57 miles per second, the bowshock encounter could damage the Probe.

The Probe needed to achieve 55 miles per second in order to safely encounter the outer gaseous bow shock wave.

Esthrep's nuclear engines had shut down from the thirty day past burn with only five percent of it's nuclear fuel remaining.

If timed just right, Esthrep had it calculated that if it fired all three nuclear engines, approximately one hour before bow shockwave encounter, that the engines would burn for forty eight seconds and achieve a slow down speed of 55 miles per second.

That would be the required speed for Esthrep to pass through the bowshock wave safely and survive.

Esthrep adjusted all of its commands and remaining resources to make it happen.

Crew again in stasis mode Esthrep controlled the probe in it's attempt to slow down.

Ten seconds later the reversed probe spat fire out of it's nuclear engines. The rumble of the engines vibrated the Esthrep orb as it monitored their speed and watched the speed calculator click down to just under fifty five miles per second at the silence of the engines.

They were ten minutes away from the bow shockwave. Their speed was correct and their vector was to enter twenty five degrees above the inner Oort cloud.

Sensors detected the wave ahead that consisted of highly charged solar wind particles.

Esthrep had engaged its forward shield and suddenly that was a tremendous shock as the wave struck the probe head on and rattled the Esthrep Probe to its core.

The Probe shook violently as Esthrep struck the outer bow shock wave. Fiery wakes of hot plasma engulfed around the forward shields just ahead of Esthrep Main's 5 meter diameter globe's position.

Esthrep could sense the heat that the shield's were unable to deflect but deep in it's programming, it was embedded that Esthrep would remain calm no matter what occurred. Five more harried minutes passed and then the Probe burst though to calmness and silence.

All around the probe they could see the Oort clout with thousands of ice asteroid bodies orbiting the sun in the outer solar system.

Esthrep could detect all the planetoids that orbited the sun in it's outer solar system.

Pluto was still fifty astronomical units away being that one astronomical unit was approximately ninety three million miles.

The probe had used up nearly all of it's resources and fuel for deceleration. The Esthrep probe was now at the mercy of gravity and momentum of it's fifty four mile per second speed.

All the probe had left were small gas guidance nozzles that could possible slightly guide the craft in small adjustments to its course.

Esthrep had made it back to the solar system but now it's challenge was to calculate a way to save the probe and somehow get it back to Mars base.

At this rate of speed Esthrep was still ten earth months away from Mars base and that was if it could somehow manage to use the outer planets as a gravity slingshot to guide it towards home.

Esthrep desperately sent a probe ahead to notify the officials of their arrival. The emergency beacon probe hopefully would inform Mars base that they had very little power and resources left and they would need a rescue in order to be captured once they had passed the asteroid belt.

The Esthrep probe was then limited to its present forward speed and present vector inward.

The forward probe that Esthrep shot was now traveling at ninety miles per second and would act as a relay and SOS beacon with the probes status and position in the solar system. Radio contact with Mars or Earth was not an option. Esthrep was so depleted it didn't have the energy required to contact real humans. It had to reserve what was left in order to use the planets gravities to possibly get near home.

With the emergency probe moving away from Esthrep, it was calculated that each minute the forward probe travel, it was almost doubling its distance ahead of the struggling to survive Esthrep probe.

In five months time, Mars base officials should receive the distress beacon from the Esthrep probe.

Esthrep coasted silently inward almost dark and powered down running only on the sixty nine percent remains of the back up fuel cell batteries on the probe. Four percent of that battery power was being used weekly to keep the six crew members safe and in a deep stasis mode. Esthrep's power consumption alone was using twice that much.

Sailing past the hearted Pluto and later Neptune,

Esthrep Main set its guidance to fall in behind the planet Uranus using the slight burst from the remaining guidance jets to chart a gravity assist that would sling the probe around Uranus towards the Planet Jupiter.

Uranus's gravity pulled the probe inward gaining speed as it grew closer to the ocean blue-green planet.

Uranus's south pole was almost pointed towards the sun so Esthrep had controlled their path to fall behind the north west side of the huge world.

A thousand kilometers above and behind Uranus, Esthrep was now traveling fifty nine miles per second and was now receiving a sling inwards behind Uranus and towards Jupiter.

Bolts welds and screws creaked and strained as the whip effect now was accelerating Esthrep around the curvature slingshot assist below Uranus.

The stress settled and Esthrep speed was as predicted now traveling at sixty eight miles per second.

The giant blue-green Uranus fell behind the probe as it now sailed a suitable path to reach Jupiter in about four Earth months time.

Planet Saturn was far away on the other side of the sun in its orbit.

Esthrep powered down all non essential power drains and vectored the ship towards Jupiter rendezvous then silently put itself into a deep stasis mode for the four month journey to Jupiter.

Three months into the sleep the probe was now under the effects of Jupiter's gravity.

The probes speed now approached seventy miles per second and in another month was expected to gain six more miles per second.

Esthrep momentarily awoke to set the finale trajectory path towards Jupiter with the chemical guidance jets and then fell back into a sleep stasis mode for two weeks time.

Fuel cell battery power was now down to ten percent. Esthrep awoke two weeks away from Jupiter as the entire planet already filled the monitor screen.

Speed now seventy one miles per second the planets gravity relentlessly pulled the probe inward at an ever increasing rate.

The crew and Esthrep were cushioned in their foam encapsulation blankets as the speeding Esthrep probe was attracted towards the back side of the humongous gas ball giant planet Jupiter.

Beginning the loop inward sling shot aboard the probe, gravity had increased to seven G forces.

For three minutes, every stitch of the probe was under stress while Jupiter exerted its mighty sling towards the asteroid belt.

Esthrep was slung out of the slingshot behind Jupiter traveling now at nearly seventy eight miles per second.

Jupiter's gravity tugged back but the probe had now gained enough speed to break free from Jupiter's gravity well influence.

By the time the probe sailed over the edge of Jupiter's gravity grip, Esthrep would be falling towards the far away asteroid belt at a speed of forty nine miles per second.

It's fuel cell batteries were now down to eight percent remaining. Esthrep had to use some of that power as it sailed away from mighty Jupiter.

In order to make it through the next few months, Esthrep would have to somehow invent resources to help the probe to survive.

Esthrep engaged solar panel that was now tuned to the suns rays but was only receiving six percent of its potential this far distance from the sun.

That power would drop to approximately six percent by the time the probe reached the outer edge of the asteroid belt.

That was just enough to slow charge the ion batteries and keep their power cells strong enough to keep the percentage from falling further.

Still not enough power to reactivate the crew, Esthrep sat alone and viciously strived by every means possible to ensure the survival of itself and it's precious crew.

The situation had become desperate. The six percent fuel cell battery charge was just enough to keep the crew safely in stasis.

Esthrep itself was using up one percent of that on a weekly basis while in the powered down alert station mode.

The far away solar rays were just enough to keep the crew alive and the batteries remaining charged at six percent.

The asteroid belt now a month away, Esthrep itself had to resort to a deeper stasis mode in order to have enough power to survive.

The sun's growing solar light was just enough to keep the power cells in balance and remain between six and eight percent.

If all went well, Esthrep would arrive at the outer asteroid belt with six percent charge remaining on the almost depleted fuel cells.

The probe now tumbled slowly towards a far away belt of half sunlit rocks and debris.

All aboard slept deeply as the blackness of space enveloped the probe that was slowly rotating but still heading in a straight line towards a specific destination.

Esthrep hibernated for several more days then reactivated a week away from the asteroid belts edge. It used it's last bit of guidance jet gas to orient the probes fixture in space.

Due to the past tumbling three months, the solar panel had only collected one percent of their potential.

Fuel cell batteries now at six percent, Esthrep had limited time to figure it's survival tactic for the next few days.

Now that Esthrep had stopped the probe from tumbling in space, it was able to focus one remaining solar panel towards the sun's rays.

That created a three percent increase and resources were still limited but sufficient to survive.

Two months away from Mars base Esthrep was basically adrift with depleted guidance jets to make any further changes to it's homeward course.

It began sending SOS messages in hopes that their forward beacon had successfully survived and informed Mars base of their dire straight situation. Sailing just above the ecliptic of the asteroids outer belt, Esthrep searched frantically for a reply to its distress message.

The probe had began tumbling again losing the resources of the solar panel.

Esthrep had used up all of it's chemical guidance jet fuel and could no longer maintain the proper orientation to harvest the solar rays.

In two weeks if not rescued, Esthrep's power would be drained to the point that it was no longer able to support life and protect the crew.

It's entire purpose was to complete that task of keeping them safe and if possible return the crew to Mars base.

Silence endured for two more weeks as Esthrep daily searched the bandwidth for a reply to its SOS.

Power now almost depleted to the amount of probe total failure.

Esthrep Main contemplated its finale chances of survival.

In thirty hours his own Orb would lose power and the crew would not survive.

Machines can't hope but Esthrep desperately continued it's search for a reply to its message of distress.

Heaters inside the probe had been deactivated in order to conserve power. Temperatures fell to below zero Fahrenheit and moisture on the inside walls had turned to ice.

Esthrep struggled with its last energy to search ahead for a rescue mission. None came that day.

CHAPTER 45
ESTHREP'S RESCUE

Cold and frozen in the stillness of space a metal clamp clasped around a ring in Esthrep's front panel.

A tug ship entitled USS Triton had been dispatched after Mars base had received the distress beacon message.

Esthrep again could feel energy surging through its circuits as the rescue ship began sharing it's energy resources through an umbilical connection.

The Crew was safe. It had been 669 years and seven months since the Esthrep probe was launched and it's data banks now contained enough information to keep the human society busy for decades.

In another six weeks the rescue ship USS Triton would arrive with the probe in tow safely at Mars base.

The probe was now being towed behind the USS Triton Rescue Tug. Technicians aboard small craft scurried around the probe to began damage scans and begin the process of accessing the recorded data.

In almost 669 years, Mars base had doubled in population and Earth had progressed much more scientifically. Now it would progress way more.

These Esthrep Chronicles that now existed were recorded in Earth's history and all the alien contacts were documented and recorded for future reference.

There would come a time in Earth's future that real humans would find a way to explore space and survive the extremes and huge distances necessary to meet aliens face to face.

But for now, the Esthrep probe had performed beautifully and decapitated any doubt that humans were alone in the universe.

Even the stars closest to our sun had intelligent life. To infer that any intelligent life form must be human looking is a thing that ones mind has to lose all doubt.

We humans may be specifically special to planet Earth but other species are just as special to their galactic situation.

Long ago as dinosaurs roamed a hot Earth, Alien civilizations had already progressed to their space age and prospered scientifically.

Earth's day would come and no doubt one day when humans were able to sustain long voyages, humans would then meet face to face with some of these alien beings.

Earthlings had already progressed a long way towards teraforming Mars.

Now, it had a commitment from contacts with the Cratts and Drogs to help in the future to try to fix the damage that their long ago war had done to planet Venus and Mars.

If you can imagine a repaired Venus that will one day support human life, then there is hope for many worlds to be explored and colonized.

That's always been this writer of the Esthrep Chronicle's dream.

It could be yours as well.

Until our paths cross. I sincerely wish you a happy planet Earth voyage no matter which ship you ride.

It's a journey we all endure until the time comes to return to the universe of stars of which we all are made from star dust.

I am yours to wonder with.

ABOUT THE AUTHOR

Full Name, Donald Eric Wilkins But ! I have always gone by Eric Wilkins my entire life and I always will.

Born, 1157 pm December 24, 1950

Henderson N. C.

Loved Astronomy from early age.

Lived many years on this Fantastic Spaceship Earth.

My Bucket List is almost full and I will soon go on to explore the Universe.

The Earth is moving toward Leo at the dizzying speed of 390 kilometers a second. That's a little over 242 miles per second.

You're on it too. God speed !

www.ingramcontent.com/pod-product-compliance
Lightning Source LLC
Chambersburg PA
CBHW050409190726
48284CB00007BB/2493